PENELOPE AND THE WICKED DUKE

SOFI LAPORTE

http://www.sofilaporte.com

Editor: Heather Osborne.
Cover Art: Covers and Cupcakes.

❀ Created with Vellum

For Chiara. The Most Original Girl Of The Universe.

CHAPTER 1

MISS HILVERSHAM'S SEMINARY FOR YOUNG LADIES, BATH, 1820

*J*ust before the first pale streaks lit up the grey morning sky, a gangly youth scrambled out of the top window of Miss Hilversham's Seminary for Young Ladies in Bath.

His feet sought support against the brick wall as he dangled precariously, clinging to a makeshift rope made of knotted linen sheets. His knuckles grazed the wall. Clutching the rope tightly, he dropped a few metres and jerked to a halt. His leather bag toppled to the ground. He cursed. Then, with a sharp intake of breath, he let himself fall.

He rolled onto the grass and listened—but the house remained quiet. He hastily collected the items that had fallen out of the bag and squashed a mangled top hat on his head. Sucking on his grazed knuckles, he crawled under the bushes to the neighbour's garden. The house had been empty for months. He opened the iron gate with a creak.

After a furtive look left and right, the boy scurried along the road and disappeared.

Just as the church bell chimed four, a man wearing a massive greatcoat and carrying a lantern and a stick sauntered around the corner from the other end of the street—the night watch.

He threw a probing glance up at the stern, grey mansion house with the Palladian portico. Yawning until his jaw cracked, he proceeded to stroll down the street.

Everything was in good order in Paradise Row twenty-four.

MISS PENELOPE SHAKTI REID, KNOWN TO HER FRIENDS AS simply Pen, sat in a mail coach to London, her heart thudding violently in her ribcage. She did not know whether that was because she was about to see Marcus soon, or because she'd just run away from Miss Hilversham's Seminary for Young Ladies, disguised as a boy. She was finally on her way to London. Alone.

Had she completely lost her mind?

Remember, you're a man now, she told herself, untucked her legs and sprawled them out widely in what she hoped was the indolently languid, masculine fashion of occupying more space than was necessary. Judging from the irritated look from the woman with the cabbage basket who sat next to her, who shuffled aside to avoid their thighs touching, she may have succeeded.

Pen's coat stretched too tightly across her chest. The trousers were too short, and that annoying top hat kept falling over her eyes. Sally, the maid, had miscalculated her size when she had procured her the clothes. She'd cut her hair earlier in roughshod fashion, leaving it long enough for her to tie together at her neck. The shears she'd used had been blunt, and her short black hair stuck out in all directions. She'd stared at her narrow face in the dim mirror and blinked. The short hair, which she'd chopped off beneath her ears and tied back severely, made her look more masculine. Her eyes were still huge, her nose possibly too dainty, her mouth a tad too long, and there was nothing to be done about those endlessly long eyelashes. But her figure was good. Pen had always been tall and slim. She'd bound her breasts tightly with bandages and worn her corset on top. She made a dapper, if somewhat gangly, youth.

Pen tilted the hat forward, so it shadowed her face. Crossing her arms, she pretended to sleep. After the last stop she really must've fallen asleep, for when she opened her eyes, the coach drew into The Golden Cross Inn at Charing Cross, London.

PEN HAD FORGOTTEN WHAT LONDON WAS LIKE.

She did not know what was more overwhelming. The sounds, which consisted of the clattering of horse hooves, the calls of the pedlars and vendors – "Sweep!" "Two a penny!" "Milk below!" and "Four for sixpence, Mackerel!" – or the overpowering smell of the city.

Faugh! How could one breathe in this noxious air? It was a miasma of rotten meat and sweat mixed with the sweetness of freshly baked bread and candied almonds. Now and then a waft of hot air from the Thames carried the smell of fish and faeces, decay, and urine.

Pen gagged.

She stood under the black statue of King Charles I on a horse and clutched her leather bag. Gaping, she watched Charing Cross Road, the hustle, bustle, and congestion.

Which way did she have to go? Right, left, or straight on?

Someone pushed her from behind, and she stumbled over the cobbles and nearly fell into a pile of horse manure.

"Move on, boy, move on," said a man carrying a crate. "Yer standing in the middle of the street."

So she was. A coach rattled by closely, and she jumped aside.

She ducked out of the way when a chimney sweep swung his ladder into her way.

"Watch it," she said, then cleared her throat. Her voice was too high. She'd have to lower her voice and grumble more.

Pull yourself together, Pen, she scolded herself. *Anyone will know you're a clumsy country bumpkin if you continue to behave as you do. Even worse, they'll unmask you as the girl you are. Recall what you came here to do.*

Marcus. She had to find Marcus.

She drew herself up. Walk like a man. Chin up. Chest out. Long strides. With purpose and confidence.

It worked. The little newspaper vending boy jumped aside.

"*The Morning Chronicle*, sir?" he piped after her.

Pen shook her head.

Bird Street. Where on earth was Bird Street?

Pen closed her eyes. She'd memorised the entire map of London back at the school. She knew she could either take a hackney, which would be the more reasonable thing to do, or she could walk. Pall Mall, Bond Street, Oxford Street, Bird Street. It hadn't looked too far on the map. How fascinating to walk alone in the streets without having a companion or maid trailing after her. She felt the rush of an exhilarating sense of freedom. Her legs started to move.

Bath was nothing like London, she decided. Bath was a pretty country village compared to this. Bath was quiet, safe. There were fewer people. The air was better, but it was also less fascinating. London pulsed with life. It was chaotic. It was loud. It was overwhelming. It surprised her that she liked it.

As she walked down Bond Street towards Oxford Street, the area grew more and more familiar. Her speed increased, as did the thudding of her heart.

There it was, the little street where she used to live, for a short time only, so long ago. As if in another life.

She stood in front of the little townhouse.

It looked like it did before, with a grey front and a wrought-iron fence at the entrance.

With wet palms and dry mouth, she lifted the brass door knocker.

A maid opened and looked at her inquisitively.

"I am here to see Mr Marcus Smith, please."

The housemaid frowned. "There is no such person living here, sir."

Pen felt like someone knocked her over.

"M-Marcus Smith?" she stammered. "But he lives here."

The housemaid shook her head. "Sorry, sir, I've worked here only for several months. The current family who lives here is called Winterbottom." She started to close the door.

"Wait!" Pen cried. "Is there anyone else in the house you could ask? Mr Jarvis, the butler? Or Mrs Jenson, the housekeeper? Fariq, the valet? I am Pen Kumari, and I used to live here. A while ago. Is there anyone working here who would still know me?"

"If you would wait, sir. I can ask the housekeeper."

"Yes, please do."

Pen sighed in relief. If Mrs Jenson was here, everything would be good. Surely, she would remember her and take her in, and if not, at least tell her where Marcus was now. Pen could've kicked herself. Why hadn't it occurred to her that Marcus no longer lived here? Was that the reason he'd never answered her letters?

A buxom woman opened the door and looked her up and down. This was not Mrs Jenson.

"I am looking for Mr Marcus Smith."

The woman lifted her eyebrows. "Mr Marcus Smith no longer resides here."

"Would you know where he is living now?"

"I am very sorry. I wouldn't know. Mr and Mrs Winterbottom reside here. We moved in with them last year. There are no domestics from the previous occupant working here."

Pen's heart sank.

"What is your relationship to this Mr Smith, if I may ask?" the woman asked.

"He is my guardian."

"Indeed!" Her demeanour left no doubt what she thought of a guardian whose ward did not know where he lived. "It is rather odd. Letters to this Mr Smith have been arriving here with regularity. From a certain Miss Penelope Reid." The woman added after some hesitation, "You would not, by any chance, know her?"

Pen's head snapped up. "Er, yes. She is my, er, um, sister."

The woman nodded. "One moment please, sir."

She left and returned with a hemp bag and handed it to Pen. "These are all Miss Reid's letters to Mr Smith. There must be nigh a hundred of them. Would you be so kind and return them to your sister?"

Pen took the hemp bag. It was heavy.

"And tell her to write no more letters to this address."

"I will. Thank you," Pen whispered.

The woman nodded and turned to close the door.

"Excuse me, ma'am," Pen said hastily. "Can you recommend some affordable lodgings in the area?"

"Why, yes. I believe the Dancing Willow rents some rooms." She pointed down the street.

Pen picked up her leather bag, tucked the hemp satchel under her arm, and left.

She stood, defeated, in the middle of Bird Street with hundreds of letters she'd written over the years. None of which Marcus had ever read. She wished she could cry, but her eyes were as dry as the Great Indian Desert in Rajasthan. Whatever scratched her throat was merely dust from the streets.

Pen hadn't cried since that fateful night in India when her parents died. She hadn't cried since the day her entire life had been buried under rubble and stone. She hadn't cried when life had stripped her of everything she'd ever known and held dear.

She'd only survived the earthquake because Marcus had hauled her out of the rubble. She'd clung to him, choking on soot and smoke and ash, but the tears hadn't come. She'd stood dry-eyed by her parents' grave, clinging to Marcus' hand. And she certainly hadn't cried when Marcus dropped her off at her school in this foreign and damp country, even though she'd howled inside.

If she could, she'd cry and scream and holler now, in the middle of this London street. She'd throw a tantrum that would make a toddler proud; never mind that she was nearly twenty-one years old, and ladies weren't supposed to throw tantrums. But then, for now, she was no lady, but a man.

Pen found the Dancing Willow, a mediocre inn. The pale green colour peeled off the shutters, but the floor inside was swept and the tables were polished. Pen supposed it would do.

The landlady rattled off a list of rules, then handed her a key. The room was an attic room—tiny, seedy, and dark—but it was hers. It had a bed, a nightstand with a pitcher, a small fireplace, and a closet. She would not stay here long. Two, three nights, maximum.

Once she'd found Marcus, he'd surely take her away to better lodgings.

After she deposited her luggage, she ventured forth into the street again.

This neighbourhood was not unfamiliar to her.

How often had she walked here with Marcus? After they'd returned from India, she'd stayed in London for several weeks. Pen wouldn't have minded continuing her life like this. But Marcus had grown quieter and more preoccupied as the days passed.

"You have to go to school, Princess," he'd told her one day. "I can't abide governesses. But there is a seminary for young ladies in Bath that seems to have a reasonably good reputation."

She'd protested violently.

He'd insisted.

She'd sulked.

He'd been adamant.

Then he said something that took any kind of argument out of her mouth. "If you care for me, you will go to that school."

"This is blackmail," she'd said darkly.

But she'd gone. To please Marcus. She believed she'd be done with school in a few years and could then return to him. She'd believed he'd visit her once, maybe twice.

But he never did.

Not even once.

He deposited her in Bath and disappeared out of her life. He never wrote. He never came on visiting day. He never invited her to London for the holidays. How she'd spent hours after hours sitting by the window in the library, her nose pressed against the glass, waiting for his carriage to arrive. It had been her most secret fantasy that he would show up one day and take her away.

It had never happened.

She was nearly twenty-one now, and not knowing what else to do with her, Miss Hilversham had taken her on as a student teacher. She was an indifferent teacher. Teaching was not her vocation. She would inherit her father's legacy when she was twenty-five. What should she do until then? Or, for that matter, afterwards? Her life was a gawking blank.

It was all so confounding.

An odd, unfamiliar tightness pressed down on her chest, and Pen increased the pace, as if to outrun it. She ran across the street, around the curve into Bond Street—and crashed with great momentum into a hard body. Both tumbled down.

She landed on top of the other person, buffered from the hard ground, yet the impact knocked the wind out of her. Their heads clashed, and she saw stars.

"Oof," both said simultaneously.

For a moment she remained lying on top of the creature she'd so expertly felled, catching her breath.

"My dear fellow," a voice gasped underneath, "no doubt it will occur to you to remove your body from mine in your own good time."

Pen scrambled off and sat on the ground. "I apologise," she blurted out. "I didn't do it on purpose. It was an accident. Truly. Are you hurt?"

The man sat up and held his head. "You certainly have a head made of marble. Good heavens! My own seems to have split in half, and I may have cracked a rib or two while cushioning you from the ground, but otherwise I seem to be intact."

He pulled himself up with a grimace. He was a head taller than Pen. His hat had toppled off, exposing blond hair, which was now slightly dishevelled from the fall. The man's shirt points were a tad too high, his cravat extravagantly tied, his tailcoat expertly cut.

Pen gulped. This was no ordinary man. There was no doubt this was a gentleman from polite society. He was too well-dressed, too athletic. An Exquisite. A Pink of the *ton.*

"Do you demand satisfaction?" Pen blurted out. Oh dear, why did she have to say that? Clearly, her brain must be infested with maggots.

The man seemed to think so as well. He picked up his hat and stick and paused. "Satisfaction? My dear —" His eyes ran down her wardrobe, taking in her dusty, ill-fitting suit and haphazardly tied cravat. "… fellow," he ended weakly.

Pen felt a flush crawl over her cheeks.

"No doubt you are new in town?" the man drawled, raising an eyebrow. "Mister…?"

"It really isn't any of your business." Pen said gruffly. Her embarrassment made her rude.

He raised his second eyebrow. "Pardon me, but you have made it my business by fairly blowing the wind out of my sails. The last time a person managed to do that was Gentleman Jackson himself."

"And I apologised." Pen felt intimidated that he'd boxed with Gentleman Jackson, the legendary boxer. Even she had heard of him.

"So you did," the man mused, taking a pinch of snuff. He offered some to her. Pen shook her head. He pocketed his silver snuffbox. "May I not enquire about the identity of the person who's so expertly felled me?"

"Pen Kumari."

She picked up her hat and jammed it back on her head. It had been an ugly specimen to begin with, but now it was completely dented out of shape. The gentleman followed each of her moves with interest.

"Where are you from, Pen Kumari?"

He turned a pair of heavy-lidded eyes at her that somehow seemed more alert than they appeared. That simple question threw her into confusion.

"I'm from… around," she said lamely, aware that she was being unaccountably rude to the tulip.

"Around." The corners of his lips twitched. "Aren't we all? Are you mayhap from India?"

She rolled her eyes. Always the same question. Always the same assumption. Her first impulse was to ignore it. Even though her mother had been Indian and her father British, she'd never identified with either nationality. She was neither. She was both. She didn't know herself what she was. But people tended not to understand. They wanted, no, they *needed* to classify her. Put her in a box with a label.

Well, Pen refused to be labelled. But explaining that to people daily was rather tiresome.

"Bikaner," she said after a moment's hesitation. "I'm from Bikaner."

That was half the truth, but he needn't know that. She was certain he did not know where Bikaner was, and she would not tell him, either.

"Pen Kumari from Bikaner. How extraordinarily interesting." He twirled a stick with a golden handle. It was very fashionable.

Pen threw him a sharp look. Was he laughing at her?

But no. He bowed elegantly. "Alworth, at your service."

This made her feel even more uncouth. She nodded curtly. "Well. I need to go. As I said, I am sorry for the, er, accident. But no harm done."

Pen backed away. She felt his gaze pierce her shoulder blades.

She fled.

CHAPTER 2

*P*en's heart hammered as her pace slowed. What on earth had just happened? Why were her cheeks still burning? She placed her hands on them and willed her heart to stop thudding. But goodness me! That had been one of the most gorgeous men she'd ever encountered in her entire life. Except for Marcus, of course. But Marcus had never dressed as that dandy did, in tightly tailored coats with padded shoulders and a golden walking stick. He'd certainly been a prime one. So handsome and athletic. He'd also smelled nice. Clean and masculine. Of lemon and something else—

"Stop it, Pen," she growled, quenching the feeling of grudging admiration.

The man who came toward her looked wary and made a big circle around her.

Pen sighed. She looked, no doubt, like a veritable country oaf. Not only was she dressed oddly, but now she also talked to herself.

When she'd instructed Sally to procure some men's clothes, cast-offs of Sally's own brother, she'd forgotten about fashion. Her encounter with the Corinthian had made her aware that she was not dressed appropriately for this fashionable city. Not only were the trousers a tad too short, but the cut of the coat was beyond anything she'd seen here. Her hat was an abomination.

And she desperately needed a bath.

Suddenly, the whiff of chilli, cayenne pepper, and turmeric wafted through her nose. It hit her; a feeling of homesickness so strong she almost felt nauseous. Pen stopped in her tracks and closed her eyes as she deeply inhaled the scent.

Of Biryani Masala, to be exact. It came from beyond that corner. Pen's stomach growled loudly.

Following her nose, Pen stopped in front of an Indian-looking place, delight flushing through her.

"The Hindoostanee Coffee Shop. Of course! The gods are good after all."

PEN LIKED THIS PLACE. MARCUS HAD TAKEN HER HERE ONCE, possibly twice, shortly after it opened. It still looked the same, even though Mr Sake Dean Mahomet, the original owner, was long gone. The colonial-style chairs and sofas were made of bamboo cane. Round pillows were arranged on the floor on a carpet around hookah pipes, and a tiger skin hung on the wall. Indian, Chinese, and Arabian ornaments and images decorated the rooms. The entire place was an orientalist vision, to cater to the fantasies of British colonial-ists. At the moment, Pen did not care. She needed food.

Pen ordered a gigantic portion of curry with basmati rice and shovelled everything into her mouth. 'Pon her soul. It was good!

She was sitting at a little corner table, and for the first time she'd stepped into the city, highly satisfied. Curry hadn't been on the menu at the school in Bath. It had been rather unimaginative, the food there. Not bad, but, well, bland. Pen and her friends used to buy sweets and biscuits with their pocket money and have midnight picnics... how long ago that seemed.

"But this is fantastic," a voice intruded into her memories. "Who would've known this place existed? An orgiastic vision of the Orient. How utterly magnificent. Yes, do bring me some food. This one. No. Wait. That one. No. A sample of everything, maybe? What is this house's specialty? I really have to try the hookah."

Pen wrinkled her forehead in annoyance. There was something oddly familiar about the drawl. She turned around to look and ducked immediately.

Zounds. It was the dandy she'd nearly killed on the street.

She hoped he didn't see her. She could leave some coins on the table to pay for her food and creep out the other way. Dropping to her knees, she started to crawl.

"Well. What have we here?" the amused voice said above her. "My nemesis. We meet again. On the ground once more?"

She saw the bottom part of a very exquisite walking stick. Beyond that, an impeccably polished pair of leather shoes and a pair of athletic legs in strapped trousers.

Pen scrambled up with flaming cheeks. "I was picking up something. Did you follow me?"

"My dear fellow. Now why would I do that? I was hungry and looking for a place to eat. This looks prime."

It all came too glibly over his lips. What would someone like him be doing in a place like this? Pen was sure he'd been following her. But why?

"I may join you, yes?" Without waiting for her reply, he pulled out a chair and sat down. He eyed her plate with interest.

"But I've just eaten, and I am about to leave." She hadn't finished her food, however, and she still felt hungry.

"Then have dessert. Bring something—" he turned to the waiter, who'd appeared, "typically Indian for our friend here."

"The Gajrela, sir, is exquisite," the waiter said.

"Excellent. Bring a dish of that."

Turning to Pen, he said, "I am to travel to India in several months' time. It is good practice to acclimatise the palate to that country's food. What would you recommend?"

"What do I recommend?" Pen echoed.

"Yes." He threw her an amused look. "I gather as a native who's eating here you must have a particular dish to recommend. Nothing too spicy for starters, as I am not yet used to it."

Pen thought. "The Vindaloo chicken is prime. I just had it myself. Not spicy at all," she lied. She'd had Biryani, but the Vindaloo was even spicier; it was the spiciest dish on this planet, generously seasoned with chilli and garlic.

"Splendid. I shall have a dish of that." The man beamed, called the waiter, and ordered the Vindaloo.

Pen stood in front of him awkwardly. "Well. Enjoy your meal. I ought to go."

"You are always in such a hurry," he complained as he leaned back, steepling his fingers, looking at her through his sleepy eyes. "Sit down." He lifted a manicured hand and invited her to sit.

Pen looked with longing at her plate. Confound it. She'd paid for the food; she might as well eat it. She tried to ignore the dandy who insisted on watching her eat with her hands, as if it were the most fascinating thing on earth.

"I have heard of this place before, of course, but never had the opportunity to visit. I see I almost missed out on a most exceptional experience."

Pen grunted. She decided the best course of action was simply to let him talk. Leaning both elbows on the table in the grossest of table manners, she tore a piece of naan, wiped her plate with it and popped it into her mouth.

"So seen in this light, I am loath to admit that I am rather grateful for you having hustled me to the ground. Even though my head did suffer for it." He placed a hand on the back of his head. "I might not have decided to try the food here if I hadn't recognised you."

"You're welcome," Pen mumbled with full mouth.

The waiter brought a bowl of water and a piece of lemon. Alworth picked it up.

"Don't drink that!" Pen exclaimed. "You're supposed to wash your hands in it. I see this really is your first time eating Indian food."

The man grinned. He really had a perfect set of teeth, Pen noted grumpily.

"The Gajrela, sir."

The waiter placed the dessert in front of Pen. Her mouth watered. This had been her favourite dish when she'd been a little girl. It was carrot pudding garnished with a gold leaf. The heady smell of cardamom almost brought tears to her eyes.

Pen picked up a silver spoon and dipped it into the orange mass. She closed her eyes in bliss. Ayah used to feed this to her. Sweet Ayah who used to tell her stories of the monkey and the crocodile, and Rama and the demon king. Then she'd tucked her into her cot and drew the mosquito net over her bed. A nightly ritual that had given her comfort. How long ago that was.

Pen sighed.

"That good?" The amused drawl penetrated through her thoughts again.

Pen's eyes popped open and looked directly into his. They

were smoky grey and deceptively sleepy. She had the impression those eyes saw more than they should. Pen shifted uneasily in her chair.

"It is quite good," she said as she popped another spoonful into her mouth.

"Excellent. I, myself, haven't had the honour of tasting any kind of authentic Indian food yet. My cook, alas, is obstinately British in his cuisine."

"You said you are travelling to India?"

"Yes. I am fulfilling—shall we say—a childhood dream of mine. I've always wanted to travel to India. And you?"

"Me?" She really did not want to talk about herself with a stranger.

"Yes, you. Pen Kumari from Bikaner, you said was your name?"

"Yes." She shifted uncomfortably in her chair. Once more, she couldn't shake the feeling that he was laughing at her, even though his face did not twitch a muscle.

The waiter brought a silver tray and placed it in front of him.

"The Vindaloo, sir."

Alworth rubbed his hands. "Ah. Here we are. This will be good, yes?"

"You have to eat with your hands." She tore off a piece of naan, scooped some of his curry onto it using her thumb and the tip of two fingers, and popped it into her mouth. Her entire mouth burned. But she did not twitch a muscle as she swallowed. She looked at Alworth with a challenge.

"Fascinating," he murmured, and proceeded to stare at his food.

"What's the matter?" Pen taunted. "Too noble to eat with your hands? Too barbaric a custom for the lofty British?"

Alworth, after another moment's hesitation, imitated her, and gingerly tore off a piece of the bread.

She watched him awkwardly stuff a heaped handful of the curry into his mouth. His eyes widened and gradually filled with tears. A dull red colour spread over his cheeks. Several beads of sweat broke out on his forehead. He swallowed and wheezed violently into the napkin he'd pressed into his face.

This was when Pen's cockiness left her. "Well. I hope you enjoy your meal. I really must go." She got up. He disregarded her and continued coughing. She edged her way out of the restaurant and ran.

Wonderful. First, she'd run him over, nearly dashing out his brains. Then she'd attempted to kill the man with curry. He'd been nice to her. He'd bought her her favourite childhood dessert. He'd wanted to converse with her. And she'd rewarded his niceness by making him eat the spiciest curry that existed on earth. Why, Pen, why?

Sometimes Pen suspected there were screws loose in her brains, indeed.

THE NEXT MORNING, AFTER SHE'D HAD A PLAIN BREAKFAST with black coffee and dry toast in the coffee room below, Pen studied her pale face in the dim mirror that hung in her attic room.

A boy's narrow face stared back at her, with a pointed chin, big, dark eyes and a generous mouth. She recoiled.

This wasn't her.

Had she made a terrible mistake disguising as a boy and coming to London? Should she have done so as a woman? But no. She would have been awfully limited in her movements. A woman alone on the streets of London? Unthinkable. No, the charade was necessary. It was also safer. For as long as she was going to be in London alone, it was better to do so as a man. The freedom of being able to do whatever she wanted was too delicious. No chaperones, no petticoats, no sitting around sewing, simpering, and twirling sunshades.

She frowned at her image. "Plan B, Pen. Plan B." The problem was that she did not have any Plan B. There was only Plan A.

Find Marcus. Marry Marcus. Live happily ever after with Marcus.

Simple, and to the point.

Now there was an obstacle to the first leg of her plan.

Marcus had disappeared.

She could, of course, turn to her very good friend, Lucy, the Duchess of Ashmore. Who had a mansion in Grosvenor Square and who, no doubt, would be more than willing to help her find her elusive guardian. Knowing Lucy, with her energy and resourcefulness, she'd single-handedly overturn every single cobblestone in London until they found him.

Except Lucy was currently residing with her family in Ashmore Hall in Oxfordshire. Even if she were here, she'd promptly put her back into petticoats and drag her from one ball to another. Because she was a duchess, and this is what duchesses did. And Arabella, her friend and Lucy's sister-in-law, who also happened to be a duchess, would introduce her to one duke after another. For her to marry.

It was a running joke among her friends that they would all marry dukes. It was, they said, fated. Three of her friends had already done so. All because Arabella had, years ago, thrown four copper farthings into a Celtic wishing well, one for each friend, wishing for each of them to marry a duke.

But Pen would never marry a duke. She'd been already back then, pig-headedly determined to marry her guardian, who was not a peer. So, she'd clambered after her coin and promptly fallen into the well, dragging down Arabella with her....Things had taken their toll from there. Lucy was expelled...and somehow ended up marrying her duke anyhow. As did Arabella. Last thing she'd heard, her friend Birdie had married a duke in Scotland as well.

Pen snorted. Coincidence. A fluke, a happy stroke of luck for her three friends. She was happy for them, from the bottom of her heart. But this fate was not for her, thank you very much. She needed no season, no husband hunting, none of the things the ladies customarily did to find themselves shackled in a ducal golden cage.

Her eyes fell on the letters strewn across her bed. Last night, she'd reread each letter and fallen asleep over them. They were repetitive, maudlin letters, and Pen was relieved Marcus had never read them.

Nonetheless, it stung that he hadn't received a single missive she'd written with such painstaking care. Each letter asking when he would come visit, when she could finally come and live with him. Not that she'd been unhappy at the seminary; not at all. She loved her friends Lucy, Arabella, and Birdie. She loved Miss Hilversham, the headmistress, who hid a kind, understanding heart behind her strict facade.

After a moment's hesitation, she gathered the letters, threw them into the fireplace and watched them burn.

How old had she been when she'd first fallen in love with Marcus? She'd been a child. Nine? Maybe ten. Marcus must've been, she calculated, twenty-five. Maybe twenty-six. Maybe older? In truth, she didn't really know his exact age. She just knew she loved him. Had loved him ever since he'd strolled into her life that hot Indian summer day. She'd been crying because—she couldn't even remember why. Was it because her kitten had run away? Back then, she'd still been able to cry over minor things like that. What a baby she'd been.

Then a gorgeous man with black hair, green eyes, a dimple in his chin, a cheeky smile on his face, had sauntered into the courtyard, hands in pocket. "Hello, Princess," he'd said, as if they'd known each other for ages. He'd shown her card tricks, and made a coin appear from behind her ear, only to toss it into the air to make it disappear again. He'd made her laugh.

He sat with her on the floor of the yard, cross-legged, and taught her how to play vingt-et-un, patiently explaining to her the rules. She'd loved him fiercely ever since.

"Where did you learn to play ving-et-un so well, Marcus?" she'd asked him, after he'd beat her for the third time in a row.

"At White's, of course." She watched his slim fingers shuffle the cards.

"What is that?"

"A men's club in London. Nothing for you, Princess. Now. Do you want me to teach you how to play picquet?"

White's.

Staring into the attic room's mirror, Pen's eyes widened. She slapped her forehead. Of course. Why hadn't she thought of this before?

She would find Marcus at White's!

CHAPTER 3

*P*en gulped as she inspected the Palladian facade of London's oldest, most exclusive gentlemen's club on St. James's Street. The crème de la crème of the *ton* frequented this place. It was the ultimate domain of men. Not a woman had ever set her foot inside that forbidden place. It was simply unheard of.

Little did they know, a woman was about to breach those hallowed grounds. Even if she had to do so disguised as a man.

Pen braced her shoulders, threw her head back and strode up the stairs, heading purposefully towards the oaken door, when someone stepped in her way.

"Where'd you think you're going?" A bulky man in a rough greatcoat sneered.

"Inside." Pen lifted her chin and attempted to push herself past him. But the man refused to move.

"This," the doorman said, nodding his chin at the door, "is a gentlemen's club." He emphasised the word 'gentlemen'.

"I am aware of that."

Once more, Pen attempted to push past him. In vain. The man was as immovable as the statue of King Charles.

"And you, clearly, are no gentleman." He crossed his arms and planted his legs apart.

"How dare you imply such a thing," Pen spat. She pulled her hand into a fist to smash into his smug face, but he caught it easily with one hand. Then he grabbed Pen by the collar, and she found herself dangling a foot high from the ground.

"Let me down!" She managed a strangled cry as she kicked about helplessly in the air.

"As you wish."

He let go. Pen crashed in an inelegant heap on the ground.

She swore.

The doorman did not heed her. He'd turned around and bowed to someone who was standing in the doorway.

Pen scrambled up and patted the dust off her pants. Through the open door, she saw a flash of scarlet on the marbled floor, stately columns, white panelling on the walls, and crystal chandeliers. She could make a run for it—she could dash up the stairs and—dash it, a gentleman obfuscated the view.

"My dear—fellow." There was an undercurrent of amusement lacing the familiar voice. "We meet again. This does tend to become a habit. Did you run over an unsuspecting victim again?"

"You!" Why was he always appearing when she least expected it?

"Do you know him, my lord? He tried to weasel his way inside. Then he tried to give me a planter. Felt like the nudge of a puppy's muzzle against my hand."

"Indeed." Alworth's voice turned haughty. "I am surprised you did not recognise this man."

"Recognise him? As the gutter rat he is?"

"Watch your words. He is royalty."

The doorman barked a laugh. "Royalty? Surely you jest, my lord."

Alworth regarded Pen with hooded eyes. "Yes, he is royalty," he said softly.

Pen blinked.

The doorman gasped for air.

"This youth is the offspring of the Maharaja of Bikaner. Are you not?"

Pen felt like someone pulled the rug off under her feet, except she wasn't standing on any rug but on dirty London cobblestone. She snapped her mouth audibly shut.

"Yes. Yes, I am." She cleared her throat. "The Maharaja of Bikaner was my grandfather." Her voice was husky. She felt the goosebumps form on her arm as she uttered the words.

"So, I ask you, man," Alworth turned to the doorman, "are you going to leave the Prince of Bikaner on the doorstep, causing a diplomatic scandal of proportions that haven't been seen before, or are you going to let him in?"

"But—but—" blubbered the doorman. "He's not a member."

"I'll vouch for him."

"But he needs to be elected, the protocol—"

"Damn the protocol," Alworth said pleasantly. "I said, I will vouch for him. I'll be his sponsor. Or do you doubt my word?" His voice took on an iron note. "Are you going to let him in?"

"No, my lord. I mean, yes, my lord. I mean, I do not doubt your word." The poor doorman, entirely befuddled, stepped aside with a deep bow.

Thus Pen, suddenly elevated to royalty, climbed up the stairs and entered the hallowed grounds of White's.

Alworth sauntered over to the hall porter, who stood to attention in his lodge.

"He is to be entered in the books. I will make sure to get the necessary signatures," Alworth told him.

"But," the porter looked at Pen horrified, "his attire!"

"Indeed." Alworth's eyes roved over her clothes once more. "His attire." He sighed.

Once more, a flush spread over her cheeks. "What's wrong with my attire?" She jutted out her chin.

He tutted. "Everything, my boy. Everything." Turning to the porter, he said, "Procure a coat."

The porter looked like he was about to cry. "Yes, my lord. But it's not only the coat."

"I know, good man, I know. But a coat will have to do for now."

"Yes, my lord."

The porter brought an elegant tailcoat of the finest material, of excellent cut, that even Pen, who had no sense of fashion, recognised it must be worth a considerable sum. Pen discarded her own coat and slipped it on.

Alworth flicked away an imaginary speck of dust from her shoulder, adjusted the collar and tightened her neckcloth. "It will do," he said and ushered the somewhat bemused Pen into the depths of London's most exclusive gentlemen's club.

Lord Archibald Edward Ainsley, Viscount Alworth, felt unholy amusement well up inside him as he leaned back in his leather armchair in White's morning room, one exquisitely booted leg extended, in one hand swirling a glass of brandy, as he studied the awkward youth in front of him. As far as he knew, he'd just helped the first woman to be a member of White's. The devil in him found this immensely amusing. He hadn't been entertained like this in ages. But then again, he had been told by more than one person he had a rather peculiar sense of humour. No doubt they were right.

Mind you, not that she knew that he knew she was a woman. And not that anyone else would discover that so easily, either. He had no interest in revealing her identity any time soon. It was too amusing to allow it all to unfold on its own. Pen Kumari looked convincingly like a youth, for all that's worth. She behaved accordingly. She sat in a chair opposite his, her head turning in all directions, her eyes big as saucers, as she took in the paintings on the walls, the mahogany tables, the scarlet carpet of the morning room. She had good legs, a tall, straight bearing, a narrow, pointed face and sharply defined, stubborn chin. Minus the stubble, of course. Her black hair was hideously cut and escaped from the hastily tied queue in her neck. There was nothing in her appearance that betrayed her as a woman. Other than her atrociously tied cravat and her poorly designed coat. Alworth suppressed a shudder. But then, there were many belonging to the male specimen who ran around in worse attire.

One would have to do something about that, he mused. A new haircut, a freshly tied cravat, and those boots, by Jove, were a crime in and of itself... but one step at a time.

He'd never have discovered her identity, he'd never have noticed her at all, if she hadn't smashed into him the moment he'd stepped out of his favourite tailor's shop. One moment he was standing, the other he found himself flattened on the ground, with her virtually bouncing off him. In that process, one couldn't help but notice, well, certain womanly curves. Despite cleverly tied bandages, corsets, and trousers.

Alworth suppressed a grin. He'd been intrigued by her from the very first.

He'd followed her to the Hindoostanee Cafe. She'd been

right that he'd been following her. And he'd discovered another intriguing piece of her identity right there and then.

"How did you know?" She turned her huge eyes on him. They were beautiful, luminant eyes fringed with long, curling lashes.

"How did I know what, child?" He met her gaze and took a sip of his brandy, taking note of the proud tilt of her chin.

"That my grandfather was the Maharajah of Bikaner." She spoke in a low voice, as if she did not want anyone else to hear. "And don't call me child."

"You yourself told me." He set down his glass to refill it.

She was highly intelligent. One had to give her that. He wondered what prompted her to run around as a man. What secrets lay behind those beautiful dark eyes of hers?

Alworth lifted the decanter and offered to refill her glass. To his amusement, she'd taken a sip, pulled a face, then poured the contents into the plant next to her when she thought he wasn't looking. He wondered how many glasses she'd pour there throughout the duration of the afternoon. Four, maybe five?

He'd place a bet at five.

He watched how a frown folded itself on her smooth forehead. "In what way did I tell you?"

"Kumari of Bikaner."

He bit down a smile. She really thought he was born yesterday, did she? Bikaner was a city in Rajasthan that he had plans on exploring.

"I did tell you I was to travel to India in several months' time, so naturally I studied the history and culture of the country. Some basic Hindi as well. My knowledge of it is, admittedly, execrable. But Kumari, or rather, Raj Kumar—it means prince, yes? Prince of Bikaner."

There was a hint of alarm in her eyes. "I didn't think that anyone would know this."

He felt the devil of an imp to tease her, so he leaned forward. "Kumari can also mean damsel, I daresay." In fact, it was the more precise meaning of the word. Unmarried girl, damsel, princess ...

She paled.

He took out a cheroot and offered it to her. He saw the denial on her lips. Then she braced her shoulders, reached out her hand—she had long, tapered fingers—and took it.

He watched in anticipation what she was going to do with it.

She rolled it in her hand, clueless what to do next.

"Kumari was my mother's name," she muttered.

Ah. Indian mother, and very likely, British father, he presumed. He was wondering why she didn't take on her father's surname. Who was she? What was her story? The mystery!

He offered her fire. She took a quick draw, coughed, and blinked her watery eyes.

"Is there a register here?" she asked out of the blue.

He paused in lighting his own cheroot. "Register?"

"You know. A book with names. Of all the members who are in the club. And their addresses. Where they live."

"Naturally. The White book of members is legendary." He blew out the smoke with great satisfaction and cherished the illicit feeling that he was smoking in the presence of a woman.

She pressed out her cheroot in the ashtray with more force than was necessary. Shame, for the cheroot was of excellent quality. "There is someone I am looking for."

"Who are you looking for?"

She visibly struggled with an answer. He saw mistrust flare up in her eyes.

"My dear Kumari. If you want me to help you—"

"I never asked for your help." She jutted out her chin.

He sighed. "No. I suppose you did not. No doubt you must have realised that without my help you would've never made it into here."

He gestured to their surroundings. "I must admit, I am keen to learn what the reason for your adamant insistence is to become a member at White's—aside from the obvious ones. So, you are looking for someone. You might as well let me help you with it."

Her face shut down. It couldn't be clearer that she trusted him as much as the mouse trusted a cat. Not that he had the intention of harming her. He was motivated by—well, what exactly was it? The alleviation of boredom? Wasn't that what motivated any of his decisions lately? He'd decided to go to India because he was bored with it all. English society. English food. England. The infernal rain. Everything was so damnably bland.

Now here was a youth—a woman in boy's clothes, to be precise—who was as un-English as a woman could possibly be.

She fascinated him.

He couldn't recall the last time he was fascinated by anyone. Yet he felt himself compelled by something more than just the alleviation of boredom. He could not yet identify what it was.

Her face, an open book, reflected her inner struggle. "I am looking for Marcus Smith," she finally said.

He lifted a finger and summoned a footman. "Check the books for a Mister Marcus Smith."

The footman scuttled away.

Pen gaped.

"Yes, it is as easy as that."

Alworth refilled her brandy glass—he counted for the third time—and mentally set a bet with himself that she'd pour it into the poor Philodendron before the footman returned.

He was right.

The moment he turned aside to fiddle with his cigar case, her hand shot out and, to his great delight, tipped the contents of her glass into the plant. She'll kill it before the afternoon was over. It was a challenge for him to keep a deadpan expression on his face.

The footman returned not five minutes later. "There is no Marcus Smith in the books, my lord."

Pen groaned. "But he must be! He said he played cards here. Most definitely. Can you check again?"

"I am sorry, sir. I am positive the name does not appear anywhere."

"But—"

"Very well. Thank you," Alworth intervened. He flipped a coin at the footman, who caught it deftly.

Turning to Pen, he said, "I must say, I spend quite a bit of my time in this club. In fact, I veritably live here. I have never had the pleasure to encounter a Mr Marcus Smith in the last fifteen or so years I have been a member here."

"I don't understand it." Pen tore at her already dishevelled hair. "Now what am I to do?"

"May I enquire as to who this Marcus Smith is? Since you assume him to be a member here, he must be a gentleman of quality. Is he a relative?"

"He's my guardian."

"Guardian! Well." Alworth digested this piece of information. "He certainly doesn't seem to take his duties as a guardian very seriously."

Pen sat up straight. "He is the best guardian in the world! There is none better."

"Indeed." Alworth raised his eyebrows. "You don't say. Aside from the fact that you've misplaced your guardian and don't know where to find him, do you have any idea at all what he does? Does he have an occupation? He must be residing somewhere."

Pen grumbled something.

"I beg your pardon?"

"I said, I'm not entirely sure what he does. He no longer lives in Bird Street. I thought he'd be here because he mentioned playing cards at White's. I am certain he must be in the books, and the footman did not look properly."

"How excessively odd." Alworth put out his cheroot, deep in thought. "Let us sum up the facts. Your quest, I gather, is to find this Marcus Smith. Who is your guardian. Who, contrary to every definition of guardianship, is quite content in leaving his charge romping alone about town. Are you even of age?"

"Not that it is any of your business, but I will come into my majority in four years."

"So you are. Additionally, this guardian of yours is being most uncooperative by not being a member of this illustrious club. Are you certain he is in London to begin with?"

Pen paled. "He must be! Where else should he be?" She jumped up and walked up and down in agitation.

Alworth admired her slim figure, her shapely legs and the manly stride she'd acquired. She also adopted the manner of pulling her hand through her hair. She made a pretty, if somewhat dishevelled youth. He wondered what she looked like as a girl. She must be quite incomparable in skirts.

As if she suddenly recalled a detail, Pen spun to look at him. "I just remembered something. He could certainly be travelling since he works for the East India Company... I think. I am not certain. He might be abroad. Maybe even in India. Then what do I do?" The look of despair on her face touched him.

"My dear boy. Sit down."

She plopped back into her chair and chewed on her fingernails.

"I propose the following. You return to your lodgings—you do have lodgings, do you not?"

To his relief, she nodded. Good. If that hadn't been the case, he'd have felt obligated to offer her lodgings in his own residence, for he had space aplenty. But knowing she was a woman, it simply wasn't the thing to do. Reputation and all that. Not that he cared too much about it, but he had been raised a gentleman. He wondered fleetingly whether her reputation wasn't already hopelessly jeopardised, since she paraded about as a man, and was now, for all men to see, in White's. Did she not care at all about it? But what did he know? She was right. It wasn't any of his business. Yet, here he was, offering his assistance. No doubt he was an idiot to inveigle himself in her problems.

"Return to your lodgings and have a good night's sleep. Tomorrow you go to the East India House to enquire whether this Marcus Smith appears in their records. And if he isn't there, how about lawyers? Banks? Someone must have a record of his guardianship over you."

Pen slapped her forehead. "Yes! Of course! Why didn't I think of it myself? I'm so stupid!" Relief washed over her face. "Of course he'd be at the East India House! And if he's not, they'd have records. That's a fantastic idea, my lord."

"My friends call me Archie."

She gaped at him.

"And you are Pen."

"I—I can't call you Archie!" A streak of red crossed her cheeks. "We're not friends."

Under normal circumstances, he'd have gladly agreed. He tended to keep his acquaintances on the superficial side. But the devil in him prompted to reply: "Are we not?"

Her flush deepened. "You barely know me."

"Very true. Who are you, Pen Kumari?"

She tugged on her ear and shrugged. "I can't call you Archie," she repeated instead of answering his question.

"Archie is better than Archibald, the unfortunate name my parents insisted on bestowing upon me. Though, you can call me Alworth if you must. And do you prefer I call you Kumari, instead of Pen?" He suppressed a grin. Princess. Damsel. It suited her.

"Pen is fine," she said hastily.

"Well then. Now that things are settled as to how we address each other, I daresay I will meet you here tomorrow at the same time and await your report. And if there is anything you need, anything at all, here is my card." He handed her his card, which she took after some hesitation.

He got up and slapped her on the back. She hadn't expected the slap, so she fell forward and caught herself before staggering into the already mistreated Philodendron.

Alworth flashed his teeth at her.

Pen visibly struggled with herself. "Yes sir. My lord. Archibald. Archie." She cleared her throat. "Alworth. Thank you."

He nodded. "Oh, and Pen. Very bad trick that you played in the Hindoostanee Cafe. That curry you made me eat was from hell's kitchen. I saw stars for a good five minutes. I should call you out for it."

She looked at him with innocent eyes. "Oh. Did you think that was spicy?"

"Go to blazes, Pen," he said peacefully.

CHAPTER 4

The East India House, the headquarters of the East India Company, was impossible to overlook. It was an intimidating, grey, neoclassical building with Doric columns that dominated Leadenhall Street.

Pen climbed the marble staircase between the columns and felt her pulse quicken.

In the vestibule, a bored-looking gentleman stood behind a standing desk. "Your purpose?" he asked, without looking up.

"I am seeking information on a gentleman who—"

"Third floor, second room. Next?"

A man behind her pushed her aside. Pen wrinkled her forehead. One thing she noticed since she was a man: people touched her more. She was forevermore being pushed, hustled, slapped, and jostled. All this physical contact took a while to get used to.

Pen found the room and confronted another clerk. He wore a harassed expression. "Purpose of visit?"

"I am seeking a gentleman who—"

"Wait in the room on the left." He pointed at a wooden

panelled room with chairs along the wall. "You will be called."

Pen sat down.

People hustled about with papers under their arms.

There were offices in the corridors to the right and left.

Pen waited. And waited. And waited.

Now and then people were called by a tired-looking, bald clerk, and they disappeared behind a green-coloured door. Pen wondered when it was her turn. She'd been waiting for a good one and a half hours already.

"You cannot, in all seriousness, ask me to wait," a nasal voice said in a complaining manner. "I will talk to your superior. This won't do. This won't do at all."

A gentleman with a haughty expression on a florid face minced into the room. His eyes scanned the room, fell on Pen for one second and looked at the empty chair next to her.

Sniffing and wrinkling his nose, he moved his chair away from her, sat down at the edge, tapping his stick on the floor with an impatient rat-tat-tat.

Pen threw him an irritated look.

The bald clerk entered again. "Where are we? Who is next?"

Pen was about to raise her hand when the gentleman got up. "This would be me, no doubt." He ignored Pen entirely.

Outrage flushed through Pen. "No, it's not. I've been waiting here for over an hour. You came in barely five minutes ago. It's most certainly my turn."

She'd let that man go first only over her dead body. He had to wait his turn like everyone else.

The man completely ignored her. "Lead on," he told the clerk, who looked bewildered from him to Pen and back again.

"I am talking to you, man," Pen hurled at him.

"Did you hear something?" he asked the clerk. "Methinks there are flies in this place buzzing about my ear. Most inconvenient."

Ice cold fury shot through Pen. "Corny-faced pig-widgeon," she muttered under her breath.

The gentleman whirled around. "What did you just say?"

"I said, corny-faced pig-widgeon." Pen stared doggedly into his face.

A dull red crept up his neck. Now his neck was red in addition to his head. "You... you... insolent pup!" He gasped for air. "Do you know who I am? My name is Blackstone. Lord Blackstone."

Pen shrugged. "Bah. I neither know nor care."

He spluttered.

She turned to the clerk. "I insist it is my turn now."

"It appears some clodhoppers still need to learn appropriate habits of this country and learn to defer to their betters," he said with a sneer at the clerk. "'Twas well done of us to introduce some much-needed civilisation to these savages."

The clerk drew himself up stiffly and faced him. "I do believe it is true that this gentleman here has been waiting for over an hour." He nodded at Pen. "I believe you are next."

Blackstone jabbed a finger at Pen. "I will remember your face." He turned to the clerk. "Yours as well." He stormed out of the room.

The clerk ignored him. "Follow me, please."

"Thank you," Pen said breathlessly, as she hurried after him down the hall. "I hope he won't make any trouble for you. He seems to be the choleric, unpleasant sort of man who enjoys causing trouble for the sake of it."

"Never fear. We have to deal with people like him daily." He hesitated before adding, "I lived in India for over twenty years. In fact, my wife is Indian." A small smile flitted over his tired face. "Alas, she isn't finding it easy adjusting to life in London."

He opened the door to an office and ushered her in. It held a desk and shelves which were crammed with papers and ledgers. He pointed to a chair.

"Now. How may I help you, sir?"

THE EAST INDIA COMPANY HAD NO RECORDS OF ANY MARCUS Smith in their employ. No book, ledger, register, or record held his name in any sort of function. He had never worked there, period. Only the passenger book held an entry that a Mr Marcus Smith, together with his valet, Fariq, and his ward, Miss Penelope Reid, had crossed on the *East Indian* from Bombay in Spring of 1814, but there was no further information other than what she already knew.

"There is nothing more I can do for you, I am afraid." The clerk closed the leather book. He threw her a sympathetic look.

Pen sagged back into her chair. "Can I ask you something? Where would I go to find a person in London? If I didn't know where they lived or worked?"

"If you ask me, it is like finding a needle in a haystack. Especially with that name. Smith." The clerk shook his head. "You might try the Bow Street Runners. We have thousands of Smiths living in this city. It is impossible on your own. I am very sorry I could not be of more help." He took off his glasses again and looked at her through pale blue, watery eyes.

Pen's shoulders slacked. "Thank you for your help, nonetheless."

. . .

PEN RETURNED TO HER LODGINGS AND FELL ONTO HER BED exhausted, with her boots on.

This Lord Alworth had suggested lawyers and banks. However, she did not know who Marcus's lawyer was. She remembered overhearing Miss Hilversham mentioning once that the Bank of London regularly transferred her tuition fees.

She'd have to visit the bank on the morrow.

However, the next day, Pen did not accomplish anything at the Bank of London either. When she exited the stately building on Threadneedle Street, she was close to giving up the search for Marcus and returning to Bath.

She returned to the club to wait for Alworth. After all, he had said to meet her there. She ordered a glass of seltzer and sat down in one of the leather armchairs facing the fireplace.

She closed her eyes and tried to call up an image of Marcus' face and found she could no longer recall the precise features. It was blurry, vague. Instead, the smirking blond image of Alworth pushed itself forward. His smoky eyes confused her, the perpetual grin on his face infuriated her, and he was clearly a dandy and good for nothing who had nothing else in his brain other than the colour of his waistcoat and the cut of his boots. He had also gathered a surprisingly correct amount of knowledge on Indian geography, besides a smattering of Hindi, Pen grudgingly admitted. He was more intelligent than he led on. She did not know what to think of him.

He'd asked her to call him Archie.

She felt herself flush.

Why had he followed her to the Hindoostanee Cafe? Why had he helped her into White's?

He had been enormously friendly to her, vouching for her at White's. Pen frowned. She mistrusted people who were overly friendly. What was his motive? What did he want from her?

A group of men entered. They were dressed in the pink of fashion and slightly drunk, even though it was not even noontime. Pen picked up a newspaper and slouched lower into her leather armchair, hoping they'd ignore her.

"'Pon rep, Forsythe's wager was beyond the pale. 'Tis a shame he lost. What shall we bet upon now?" The man who uttered this took a big gulp from his brandy glass and belched.

"A bet, a bet! I have one. Here it is. Let us bet that there ain't but twenty curricles a minute that drive down St. James's—"

"Boring!" the other men interrupted in unison.

"Really, Pennington. Must you be such a bore? Counting curricles indeed. I have something better," a booming voice said.

Pen sat up. There was something familiar about the voice. Where had she heard it? She peeked around the chair cautiously to catch a glimpse, then spun back and sunk lower in her chair.

Zounds, the bulky man with the red face was the corny-faced pig-widgeon! What was his name again? Lord Black-ware, Blackstore. Blackstone!

He was speaking now. "Let us bet the Duchess of—who's this starchy prick in Parliament—ah, yes, I remember—Ashmore—would you believe this, gentlemen: the Duchess has a scarlet past! Was said to be an actress before she married him. Heard it myself from an opera dancer who stood with her on stage not three years ago."

Pen dug her fingernails into the armrest as she realised he was talking about her best friend, Lucy, the Duchess of Ashmore. She held her breath as she turned to look again.

"So the Duchess of Ashmore's a light piece of muslin, a

doxy. Once a doxy, always a doxy. Get my meaning?" Blackstone wagged his bushy eyebrows at them.

"I don't know, Blackstone. Wouldn't want to cross Ashmore." The man called Pennington weighed his head back and forth. "Damn powerful man, he is. Said to love his wife."

"You're a bore, Pennington. If he loves her, make the stakes even higher." Blackstone slapped his hand on the table. "Let's bet any of us can get under her skirts within–say—give and take—two months, three? They're all the same, actresses, doxies." He waved a dismissive hand.

Forsyth slapped his thigh with a hooting laugh. "Aye! You do come up with the best ideas. That's prime. Get the betting book!"

"How dare you!" Pen shot out of her seat, pale, wrath shooting out of her eyes.

"Eh?" The three men looked at her, nonplussed.

"How dare you! Insulting the Duchess of Ashmore in this lewd manner, slandering her reputation and honour. What did she ever do to harm you that you must talk about her in this utterly vile way!" Pen clenched both fists and trembled with rage.

"Who is this milksop?" asked Forsyth.

"You! I recognise you!" Blackstone wagged a fat finger at Pen.

"You know him?" Pennington, too, had risen from his chair.

"Demme, if that isn't the insolent whelp from the East India House. Calling me vile names, even as he does now! What did you call me then? Eh?"

"Corny-faced pig-widgeon!" Pen hurled at him. "And so you are! All of you! You are no gentlemen. You are nothing but a bunch of evil bell swaggers."

"Now look here, no one is calling me a bell swagger." An angry flush coloured Forsyth's cheeks.

"If you take the liberty to insult my friend, then I take the liberty to call you a bell swagger and worse." Pen's eyes shot lightning rods at him.

Blackstone stalked over to Pen, pushing a chair out of the way.

"Just let the greenhorn be," Pennington muttered, placing his hand on his arm. But Blackstone shook it off.

"By my honour. This cannot go unpunished!" Blackstone's florid face took on a shade of puce.

Pen drew herself up straight. "Honour? You speak of honour? You have none. But my friend does. And so do I!"

"How dare you!" Blackstone spluttered.

"I say, Blackstone. Do you let that insult sit? For the second time? Ought you not to demand satisfaction from that whelp?" Forsyth asked gleefully.

"A duel." He huffed, and beads of sweat appeared on his forehead.

"Aye, a duel! I'll be your Second." Forsyth bent forward and lowered his voice. "You can best this milksop in a trice."

"Can I? Very well. Very well indeed."

"My name is Pen Kumari," Pen said it with the haughtiest tone possible. "I accept. To defend my friend's honour."

"Name your Second." Forsyth demanded.

"I, uh, don't have any."

Blackstone bared his teeth. "Then get one. Tomorrow. Hyde Park, at dawn. I will make mincemeat out of you, insolent pup." He narrowed his eyes. "And if you don't show up, I will send my men after you, Pen Kumari. Mark my words. I will remember your face and find you."

Pennington eyed her dubiously. "Do you even know how to hold a pistol, boy?"

Pen smiled contemptuously. "I'm a prime shot. I've killed tigers in India with a single shot."

"Did you hear that, Blackstone? That makes things rather interesting. Should we place a bet?" Forsyth was eager to get the betting book.

"Pah. Tigers." Blackstone threw Pen a scathing look before drawing aside Pennington. "Just because he can kill tigers in the jungle doesn't mean he can hold himself up in a duel, can he?"

"But tigers, man. Tigers! They're devilishly ferocious…"

The men left the room.

Pen collapsed in her chair.

Zounds.

Not two days in London, and she'd managed to knock out a Corinthian, squabble with the doorman of White's and call out a lord for insulting her friend Lucy.

Pen gulped.

Then she finished her drink and cracked her knuckles. She ought to be proud of herself. Her initiation into the world of men had certainly started out well.

CHAPTER 5

a duel at dawn. Tomorrow. To defend Lucy's honour. They'd insulted Lucy in the grossest manner! She still trembled with anger at the memory of their words.

She was proud to die for her friend, defending her honour, but did it have to be now? She would've liked to find Marcus first before she died and tell him... well, what?

Besides, she had no pistol.

Where did one get a blasted pistol?

Lord Alworth came to mind once more. His tousled blond hair, his grey eyes and lopsided smile. Could he lend her a pistol?

She'd waited for two more hours after Blackstone and his friends had left, but Alworth never appeared at the club. Pen pulled out the card he'd given her and squinted at the elegant, flourishing letters.

It appeared she was going to Cavendish Square.

THERE ARE BUTLERS, AND THERE ARE BUTLERS.

There are the invisible ones whom one never notices.

And there are those who are so haughty that King George himself would be intimidated.

Lord Alworth's butler belonged, unfortunately, to the latter category. He peered down his long eagle nose, making Pen feel as if she were a cockroach.

She pulled herself up. "I am here to see Lord Alworth."

He did not twitch a muscle in his face as he said, in a nasal tone, as if he had an uncured cold, "His lordship is currently not at home. You may leave your card."

She didn't have any card. She searched her pockets and pulled out a wrinkled, many-folded piece of paper that advertised the Hindoostanee Cafe, which she'd stuffed it into her pocket before her hasty departure from the cafe.

She handed it to the butler. "My name is Pen Kumari. He is expecting me. You'd better let me in."

He held it between his gloved forefinger and thumb and wrinkled his nose. "As I have said, his lordship is not in residence." The butler's voice could've frozen the Serpentine in summer.

"He will not be pleased when I meet him at his club later and tell him that his butler refused to let me in. He asked me to call on him as soon as possible." That was a white lie, but Pen figured it didn't harm.

The butler stiffened for a fraction of a second, then he opened the door. Disapproval oozed out of his every pore.

"Follow me, sir."

He led her to the drawing room with slow, measured steps, carrying her wrinkled paper on a silver platter.

Pen looked around curiously as she trotted after him.

This Viscount Alworth certainly lived in style. It was a light, friendly hall, not overly cluttered with vases and busts, but tastefully decorated in mint green that contrasted nicely with the mahogany of the furniture.

The drawing room was pleasant, with blue curtains. A big oil painting with a ship sailing on a rough ocean hung over the fireplace. Pen had barely sat down on the recamier sofa when the butler entered again and bid her to follow him up the staircase.

"His lordship awaits you here." He held a door open for her.

"But... This is the bedroom!"

With an unfathomable look, the butler closed the door behind him.

By Jove. Was the viscount in the habit of greeting his guests in bed? This was a masculine domain, and she had no business being in here.

Her eyes flew to the tremendous four-poster bed, which was rumpled and thankfully empty.

She breathed a sigh of relief. Where was he?

"Hello?" she called.

"My dear friend." His languid voice came from somewhere back.

Pen turned and espied a door that led to an anteroom. Alworth's dressing room. Here was the man himself, in bare feet and linen shirt and trousers, looking for all that was worth as if he'd just risen from bed.

Pen felt a hot flush spread all over her body.

"Ah, Pen. I see you are here." He yawned. "Do you have any idea what the time is?"

Pen looked at the clock on the mantelpiece. "It's nearly noontime, sir."

"Precisely. The middle of the night, child."

"I-I'm sorry," Pen stuttered.

She couldn't tear her eyes away from him. Alworth's hair stuck out in all directions, making him look boyish and somehow vulnerable, yet he had a definitive stubble on his chin, which was so very manly. Lawks! She ought not to stare

at him like that. He sat down in a chair and closed his eyes.
Was he falling asleep right there and then?

The valet entered with a bowl and towel and proceeded
to sharpen the razor on a leather strap.

Pen stepped from one foot to another. Was she supposed
to watch this procedure? It was rather interesting, given the
fact she'd never seen a man do his toiletry before.

The valet dried his face, patted cologne on it—Pen
inhaled it; it smelled divine—a mixture of bergamot and
lemon, and something else—a masculine smell that assaulted
her senses, simultaneously decadent and refreshing.

Then the valet handed him an apricot-coloured
waistcoat.

Alworth waved it away. "Not this."

"The blue one, sir?"

"No. Methinks the cream. Or the red." Alworth sighed.
"What a confounding decision to have to make at the crack
of dawn. What do you think, Pen? Cream or red? Since you
were the one who dragged me out of my slumber, it seems
only appropriate that you help me solve this dilemma."

"I'm very sorry, sir. If you like, you can continue sleeping,
and I'll return later."

Who slept until nearly noontime, anyway? Pen rose regularly at six.

"Nonsense. Well? Which one?"

Pen tipped her head to the side. "It depends on which coat
to match it with, I suppose?"

"Excellent point, my dear Pen. I will wear the dark blue
coat today. Together with the cream waistcoat. No. Wait. The
red striped one it shall be. Or will that clash with the tapestry
of the coffee room at White's?"

Pen gaped at him.

"What a dilemma, Pen," he moaned. "Thirty-nine waistcoats and nothing to wear."

"Forty-three," the valet grumbled.

Alworth popped an eye open. "Did you say something, Walker?"

"I said forty-three, sir. Forty-three waistcoats." He pulled out the red striped one and held it up. "And an equal number of coats. That is in addition to twenty-three pairs of pantaloons, thirty-three cosack trousers, and nearly fifty-three shirts," he said aside, so that only Pen heard him. "Not to count the cravats."

Pen snickered.

Alworth stared at the red striped waistcoat pensively. Then he waved it away. "It does remind me of the wallpaper at White's. I shall wear the pink one today."

"An embroidered one, or a striped one?"

"Pen?" Alworth massaged his temples.

"Depends on the embroidery." Pen choked.

"Walker?"

The beleaguered man sighed. "We have silver leaves, golden flowers and one with curly whorls." He made a motion with his forefinger.

"Silver leaves sound lovely," Pen contributed. "Reminds me of autumn."

Both men looked at her blankly.

"You know? Leaves falling?"

Alworth seemed to ponder on the matter. "Indeed. I associate leaves with summer."

"Spring is more likely," Walker put in unhelpfully.

"The pink silver leafed waistcoat it is, Walker. Regardless of whether it is seasonally appropriate."

"Very well, sir."

The valet helped him into his waistcoat.

Alworth stood in front of a body-length mirror and tied his cravat.

His valet stood next to him, as still as a statue, holding

various starched neckcloths in his hand. Now and then Alworth cursed and threw a cravat on the ground, held out his hand, and Walker handed him a freshly pressed one. Then the entire procedure started anew.

"I was going to ask you—"

"Shh!" The valet threw her a ferocious look. "Do not talk while he ties his cravat. It requires the utmost concentration."

Pen snapped her mouth shut.

It took Alworth several tries and several more discarded neckcloths until he was satisfied.

When he was finished, he turned. Pen swallowed. He was all the crack. He looked glorious. Even the pink waistcoat, as ridiculous as it was, muted by the dark blue tailcoat, looked good on him.

"Here is a quick lesson in men's fashion, my good Pen. Pay close heed to my words. The best way of dressing is with understated elegance. Perfectly fitted and tailored garments. Immaculate linen. Starched and pressed cravats, tied to perfection. Do you understand?"

She nodded but eyed his pink waistcoat doubtfully. Understated elegance and pink waistcoat?

The corner of his eyes crinkled as he smiled. "Here is a second lesson. Never be a follower, but a leader and creator. Especially in fashion. Be striking, but not vulgar. The colour of the waistcoat is my personal statement. My signature, if you will. Do you see my point?"

"I think so." She cleared up her throat. "May I ask a question, sir?"

"Ask away, child."

"Do you habitually have people watch you dress?" she blurted out.

"It used to be somewhat of a sport when Brummel was still around," Alworth replied.

Beau Brummel? The legendary dandy? Pen snapped her astonished mouth shut.

"His lordship had twenty people crammed into this dressing room, once," Walker grumbled. "All wanted to see how he tied his legendary cravat. But no matter how often they watched him tie it, none of them managed to reach the same perfection as his lordship."

"Thank you, Walker." Alworth lifted his hand and beckoned with one finger. "Come here."

Pen stepped forward with a frown. She jumped back when Alworth fiddled around her neck.

"Stand still, boy. You can't walk around like this. It's a disgrace."

Alworth picked up one of his starched and ironed neckcloths, tied it around her neck and folded it in some intricate manner. His knuckles brushed her chin more than once, and she felt something flutter in her stomach.

"There. Much better." He patted her shoulder. "You will find you can accomplish so much more in this world if you are appropriately dressed."

"It's rather tight," Pen stretched her neck. "And hot. I can hardly breathe."

"And so it should be, my good Pen. Tell me then, what is so urgent that you must drag me from my bed at this ungodly hour?"

"A pistol," she replied. "Do you have a pistol I may borrow?"

"Of course I do." He strolled over to a Chinese cabinet, opened the doors, drew out an inlaid mahogany box and handed it to her. "Will this do?"

She took it and flipped it open. Two pistols lay inside. Even to her unschooled eyes, the two flintlocks looked well crafted. She picked one up. The metal was cold against her hands.

"Anything else?"

"No. Thank you. That is all." She did not know what to do
with it and gestured awkwardly toward the door. "I suppose
I will leave and let you continue your, er, morning routine."

He dropped into an armchair and crossed his legs.

"You know, one needs bullets for the pistol to work," he
said conversationally.

Pen paused. "Oh." Another pause. "It's not loaded?"

"No, my good Pen. It is not. Do you know how to do it?"

She weighed it in her hand awkwardly.

Alworth lifted an eyebrow. "I gather not. What do you
need it for?"

"To shoot a bullet into someone."

"Ah yes. Silly of me to ask." He looked at her through
heavy-lidded eyes. "Who is the unfortunate fellow you need
to shoot?"

"It's none of your business."

Alworth sighed. He got up and held out his hand. "In that
case, I need to reclaim my pistol."

Pen clung to it. "I will bring it back when I don't need it
anymore. I promise."

"The devil you will. Sorry to say, whelp, that I don't
entirely trust you. How do I know you don't intend to assas-
sinate someone? With my pistol? Come, come, that
won't do."

She struggled with herself. "Lord Blackstone."

"Blackstone?" He looked at her, perplexed. "What dealings
do you have with him?"

"I have a duel. Saturday. That's tomorrow." She gulped.

"I daresay you will defeat Blackstone easily in a duel," he
said. "He isn't the best of shots." Alworth frowned. "Nonetheless, it is atrocious of him to call out a mere child."

"I'm not a child!" Pen flared up.

"Hm. That remains to be debated. He's known to be a

hideous shot. And cowardly. Anyone can best him. Even you."

Pen nodded unhappily. "Of course."

"Pen Kumari. You do know how to shoot a pistol, do you not?"

A pause. "Certainly. I've shot tigers in India with one shot." She evaded his eyes.

"Tigers." He sighed. "I see this day promises to be quite busy. Pistol practice before breakfast, I tell you. What has the world come to?"

"I did not ask for your help nor would I ever—"

He lifted his hand. "Do me a favour, Pen, and let us have breakfast before you impart to me the entire story. I'm fiendishly hungry. Come."

The latter came out as a command and allowed no counter argument. He held out his hand. Pen placed the pistol in it. He locked it away in the Chinese cabinet and motioned her to follow him to the dining room.

"I need strong coffee, and my friend here will join me for breakfast," Alworth imparted to the butler.

"Very well, sir."

"I really shouldn't disturb your breakfast like this," Pen mumbled.

"Have you broken your fast yet?"

In response, her stomach growled loudly.

"I ascertain not. Sit down."

He motioned at the chair opposite to his. The footman served them beefsteak. Far too heavy a fare for breakfast, for Pen was used to toast and tea, but as it was noontime, she was so hungry she could've easily consumed an entire cow.

After they had eaten, Alworth dabbed the corner of his mouth with his napkin and leaned back in his chair. The butler poured coffee. Alworth added four spoonfuls of sugar and milk.

"The sweeter, the better," he explained. She herself drank her coffee black.

"Now tell me exactly how it came about that Blackstone called you out."

Pen rambled off the story. "I suppose I shouldn't have insulted him. But I was so angry, you see."

"What did you call him?"

"A corny-faced pig-widgeon."

Alworth guffawed. "You're priceless, Pen. Blackstone is understandably offended."

"Yes." She looked at her coffee unhappily.

"You could back out of it. Cowardly, but it'd be the easy way out."

She sat up, stung. Her black eyes flashed. "Never. It's a matter of honour. You weren't there when it happened. How they insulted Lucy. It was unbearable! It was crude, rude, dastardly and disgusting."

He held up his hand. "Who on earth is Lucy?"

"My friend. I would die for her."

"No doubt you have set yourself up for that very opportunity. But let us backtrack one step. *Who* is Lucy?"

"The Duchess of Ashmore."

He raised an eyebrow. "Ashmore. By George. That is elevated company. What do you have to do with the Ashmores?"

"Lucy's a very good friend." Pen jumped up and walked up and down, gesticulating. "To return to the point. It isn't fair to slander a person's honour when they aren't even there to defend themselves. Granted, they were half drunk, but that is no excuse. I won't have any of my friends slandered in such a manner."

Alworth wondered whether Pen would defend him similarly, if he ever had the honour to enter her ranks of friendship. She was fiercely loyal to those she called friends.

She ranted on and on until Alworth lifted another hand. "Hasn't it occurred to you that Ashmore might be more than capable of defending his wife's honour—in a more effective, yet less dramatic, way? Has it ever occurred to you he might not appreciate you standing up for his wife? And that it might bring about the opposite effect: blowing it up to a full-fledged scandal that is even more difficult to quench?"

"I don't care a tuppence for what Ashmore thinks. I only care about Lucy's reputation."

"So you said. What about your own reputation?" His eyes bored into hers. He willed her to trust him enough to reveal the truth about who she was.

She opened her mouth, snapped it shut, folded her arms and frowned ferociously. "I don't have any reputation. And if I did, I wouldn't care a tuppence about it."

Alworth regarded her for one moment. She did not care about her own reputation but would die for her friend's. There were few men who'd do the same. "If you are determined, then, to meet him, I will help you."

Pen gulped.

"I'm certain you'll do very well." Alworth slapped her shoulder, throwing her forward so that she nearly dunked the tip of her nose into her coffee. "Anyone is able to shoot better than Blackstone. And now, to shooting practice."

ALWORTH ENJOYED HIMSELF IMMENSELY. PEN WAS, POSSIBLY, the worst shot he'd ever seen. She had no sense of aim whatsoever. Her grip on the flintlock was too low and so hard, her knuckles whitened at her clutch. She scrunched up her entire face in deep concentration and levelled the pistol. She shut both eyes, then fired.

"Did I hit it?" she asked after she opened her eyes again.

Alworth shook his head. "Congratulations. You assassi-

nated the cherry tree. You shot off an entire branch. That's
no mean feat."

"Really?" Pen beamed.

Alworth sighed. "No. I was being sarcastic. You were
supposed to hit the bullseye on the target."

The target was a good two feet to the left.

"Oh."

"Whoever stands near Blackstone tomorrow had better
write his will today," Alworth muttered. "Keep your eyes
open. Never lose sight of your target. Loosen your grip. You
need a quieter hand if you want to hit Blackstone. Not that
the fellow is easy to miss, with his dimensions."

Alworth helped her aim by moving her hand to the right.
Some strands of her hair tickled his nose. They smelled of
honeysuckle.

"Keep in mind, you want to hit Blackstone. Not his
Second. Nor, heaven forbid, the surgeon. Speaking of which.
Who is *your* Second?"

"I don't have any."

"Confound it, brat. You can't go to a duel without a
Second! I see I will have to be your Second."

"You really don't have to."

"Nonsense. Of course I have to. You are using my pistols,
after all."

Alworth made a mental note to revise his will for good
measure. It might not be such a bad idea to stay away from
Blackstone's vicinity as well. Especially when she aimed.

She looked at him sheepishly. "I am most grateful. I am
terribly sorry to inconvenience you so."

"Take another aim," he told her after he reloaded the
pistol.

She shot and hit the branch on the right, not even
brushing the target.

"There goes the surgeon," Alworth said cheerfully.

. . .

THEY PRACTICED FOR SEVERAL HOURS UNTIL ALWORTH declared it was time to go to White's.

"Is that all you ever do?" Pen asked him, as she sat beside him on the curricle. "Sleep until noon, break the fast, then go to White's to eat some more? And play cards. Must be a hard life, indeed."

"Yes, my child. And the tailor. One should not underestimate the time one needs at the tailor." He flicked an imaginary speck of dust away from his sleeve. "It is most imperative to get perfectly fitted and tailored garments."

She shook her head. "Don't you have a family to take care of?" she blurted out.

"A family?" he uttered a short laugh.

"Well, you do have a family, do you not?"

He hooded his eyes. "I have a younger brother and a sister, yes. And a gaggle of nieces and nephews. I lost count. I daresay I have an elderly aunt somewhere as well. All of us meet once a year at Christmas. Alas. After a fortnight, all of us are more than happy never to see each other's visages again, and we cannot wait to proceed with our own lives." He gripped his reins tighter than was necessary.

"I think it must be lovely to have a family," Pen said after a charged pause. There was a note of wistfulness in her voice that made him look sharply at her.

"We have nothing whatsoever in common. They tend to disapprove of me, so the less we see of each other, the better." Alworth shrugged.

"Why on earth would they disapprove of you?" She sounded so genuinely surprised, that Alworth looked at her sharply.

Alworth pondered on it. Why indeed? It hadn't always been that way. He remembered a time when he enjoyed romping about the forest with his younger brother, fishing and climbing and falling out of trees. His sister hadn't been the moralising bore she was today and tugged along after them, her chubby face smeared with the blueberries she picked. Along with Serena. His childhood love, whom he'd vowed to marry. Then their mother had died of smallpox.

Everything had changed.

His father remembered he had an heir who needed to be raised for his role as future viscount. He was separated from his siblings, playmates, even from his dog. He was expected to be an adult from one moment to the next. His beloved nanny left, and he was sent to school.

When he was barely eighteen, his father died. And Serena married someone else. He learned early on it was better to keep a distance to those he loved best. Not to get too emotionally attached to people, animals, and things. For when one was too attached to something, it led to inevitable pain. Living life on the surface was best. Pleasant and easy-going. While his brother became a vicar, and his sister married a country baron and settled down in a staid life, he joined the dandy set and befriended Beau Brummel. Boxing, fencing, and shooting, now and then some easy gambling, visits to his club and his tailor. This filled his time.

To Pen he said, "I suppose as heir, my father believed I had to be raised differently from my siblings. At first, they catered to my every whim. It caused somewhat of a rift between us. Then they shoved me off to school, where they dunked my head into the chamber pot every morning and evening. It's been most improving upon my character. In fact, one might argue that this prevented me from growing up entirely spoiled, though some people might debate that."

Pen gasped. "How terrible!"

"Children, especially a crowd of rowdy boys, can be intolerably cruel to one another. As regards my siblings, we had nothing in common and grew apart."

"It is not us who have changed," his sister Beatrice had once hurled at him. "It's you. The Archie we love has left, and you replaced him with this–this–Bond Street Beau, this charade of a dandy. You're hiding behind your waistcoats, cravats and hats. I don't know who you're trying to impress. Certainly not me."

Thus, the distance between him and his family had grown further and further. There was an unbreachable chasm between them. His sister was right. He lived in an entirely different world.

CHAPTER 6

They arrived at the club, where the porter wordlessly handed Pen a coat.

"Something occurred to me," Alworth mentioned as he strolled into the coffee room. "You mentioned your guardian plays cards? He is a gamester?"

"Yes. He is very good with cards."

"He might be frequenting different clubs. Madame Spiel's, maybe. Any gamester would try that. Or Perpignol's. But no. I suppose Perpignol's is out of your league."

Alworth lifted his finger and ordered a glass of burgundy.

"What's Perpignol's?"

"A gaming hell. That's where only the hard-core gamesters like Rochford go. No place for you, child. They'll pluck you the minute you step into the room."

"Who is Rochford?"

"Never say you haven't heard of the notorious Duke of Rochford? He is one of the most degenerate men that walk on the face of this earth. He fills the gossip columns daily." He waved a hand at the newspaper that lay on the coffee table.

Pen picked it up. Indeed, the headlines proclaimed in bold ink: 'Scandal at Perpignol – Lord V fleeced by Duke R. V dead'.

"Duke R – Duke Rochford fleeces who?"

"That would be Lord Villingham. Lost his entire fortune to Rochford in a single game." Alworth shook his head. "Shot himself, the poor sod. It's never a good idea to cross Rochford."

"That is absolutely horrifying! Poor man!"

"It's his own fault if he plays against Rochford."

"He sounds vile."

"He is. Perpignol is full of the likes of him."

Pen pushed the newspaper away. "I don't read gossip columns." She paused. "Do you suppose I should? For news about Marcus, I mean?" She picked up the newspaper again.

"Doubtful there's anything useful in the gossip sheets. Only about men shooting each over their lady loves. How a man can allow himself to get carried away over something they declare love is beyond me."

"I take it you do not believe in love?"

"My dear Pen. No. I do not. It seems to be an affectation that makes men make fools out of themselves, nothing more."

Pen digested that. "I do believe in love," she then said, "very much so." She'd been painfully in love most of her life, so she'd become somewhat of an expert on unrequited love.

"You are a romantic, then."

"A fool, more likely," she muttered. "As you say."

"Ah. Then you would very much enjoy tonight's programme at the opera," Alworth said brightly. "Mozart's *Seraglio*. It is about love and foolishness."

"Opera?" Pen shook her head. "I have a duel tomorrow morning, in case you've forgotten. I'd be better off practicing my shots."

"I beg to disagree. I firmly believe the best thing one does the night before a duel is to go to the opera. Listen to music and introspect. Mind you, not that this is a pastime I allow myself to indulge in too often. However, the night before something as momentous as a duel, music is most excellent in helping one relax."

"I'd rather stay at home tonight."

"And spend a sleepless night tossing and turning in bed? That won't do." He clapped a hand on her shoulder. "The opera it is tonight." He studied her coat and pulled a face. "However, not in this outfit."

Pen looked down at her coat. "No. This belongs to White's."

He pursed his lips. "Weston's will have something suitable for you."

Pen was inclined to argue. Then she thought otherwise. Alworth was right. She needed a new outfit if she was to quit drawing attention to herself for her shabby appearance. So she obediently trotted after him as he took her to Weston's in Bond Street.

They left the shop with an entire suit for her, including evening breeches, waistcoat, shirt, and a fine coat, which had cost a fortune, but Pen paid without blinking.

"I will send you my carriage in the evening. Where do I send it to?" Alworth looked at her expectantly.

Pen hesitated. "It really is unnecessary. I will simply meet you at Cavendish Square."

"I insist."

"So do I."

He came to a full stop. "Pen. I can't have you walk alone at night to my place. It won't do."

"Nothing will happen. I have a pistol now, and I know how to shoot." She pulled out the pistol and waved it about.

"You shoot as well as a blindfolded monkey. You'll get

plucked and eaten if you traverse the streets at night on your own."

"Bah. I hit the target three times today." She'd barely brushed it, but Pen considered it to be a feat. "I'm not afraid. Stop behaving like a mother hen, my lord. I never asked you to accompany me. This is my problem to solve, not yours."

He certainly was right. That did not make things any better.

"Very well, Kumari. Have it your way," Alworth said coolly. "We will meet at seven at the opera."

He strode away and left Pen standing on her own in the street, staring after him and feeling oddly forlorn.

CHAPTER 7

*S*he should've taken Alworth's offer to take his carriage. The problem was that she hadn't wanted him to know where she lived. It was none of his business, she told herself. She was ashamed of her lodgings, and she didn't want him to see how and where she lived.

Pen could not afford to move into the Albany, an exclusive address that provided elegant apartments for bachelors at a costly price. Pen still had funds aplenty, but she was economical about spending her money. The new set of clothes, which she'd insisted on paying for herself, had ripped a considerable hole into her savings. Who knew how long it would take her to find Marcus? Who knew how long she'd have to stay in her current lodgings?

She dressed carefully, pulling on dark blue breeches, a silver waistcoat, and a dark blue tailcoat that a customer had ordered but never bought. It fit her to perfection. Even in the dim mirror, she could see that she made a dapper young man. With wet fingers, she flicked her hair back. She struggled with her cravat, trying to imitate Alworth's movements as he'd tied his. The result was less than stellar, but it'd have to do.

Pen stepped into the street, feeling smart. She felt excitement sizzle through her as she hailed a hackney. How she looked forward to the opera! It would be her first ever opera.

She arrived in Bow Street and admired the Theatre Royal with the four fluted colonnades. Carriages stopped in front of the entrance and magnificently dressed people descended.

She spied Alworth in the foyer, talking to a lady with a purple turban, seemingly unaware of Pen's presence nearby. The woman pulled a young girl forward, who blushed, and Alworth pulled out one of his charming smiles as he bent over her hand.

For one fraction of a second, Pen wished she was her. How would it be if Alworth were to see her as a woman, bowing over her hand? How would it be if she were the recipient of that charming smile?

Alworth really looked breathtakingly splendid in dark breeches that clung to his thighs, an immaculately tailored coat, and crispy white cravat. He wore a purple waistcoat, which made Pen blink, and apparently a corset that nipped into his waist. His shoulders were broad, possibly because they were padded. His blonde hair was coiffed into careful disorderliness. He was a dandy, through and through, yet there was a wiry toughness underneath it all. A sharp awareness covered by his sleepy smile. The man inside wasn't at all like the appearance he presented to the world. Pen wondered why.

He turned heads. The ladies tittered behind their fans and threw him languishing glances. Pen felt a stab of annoyance. Silly creatures.

She shifted from one leg to another, not knowing what to do with her hands. Should she approach him? He didn't seem aware that she was there. Or did he ignore her on purpose?

He wasn't cutting her, was he? Everyone was here with someone else. Couples stepped up the vast staircase to their boxes. Should she go ahead? But then she did not know where Alworth sat, whether he had a box.

She felt foolish alone among the glitter and glamour, the elegance and grandeur. Now the silly girls had noticed her hiding behind the statue and tittered about her, hiding their faces behind fans. Pen had an unreasonable urge to check her hair in the gilded mirrors on the wall. Maybe she had a stain on her coat or a smudge on her cheek... Zounds. Did that tall girl just bat her eyelashes at her?

Pen moved closer to the marble statue, wondering whether she could hide behind it, and prayed Alworth would finish his conversation soon.

After a while, the lady left, and Alworth turned. He nodded at her coolly. Pen stepped up to him, relieved.

"Are you still angry at me? As you see, I made it here unhurt. No one tried to confront and pluck me in the streets. I am sorry I incurred your disapproval this afternoon by turning down your carriage." She lifted her shoulders. "You've already done too much for me. I suppose I simply don't like to be beholden to anyone."

Her unexpected frankness must have disarmed him. His aloofness melted. "You are not beholden to me by taking my carriage, child. It was a gesture of goodwill. Of friendship."

"Is this what we are? Friends?" She searched his face.

He lifted an eyebrow. "You don't give you loyalty easily, do you, Pen Kumari?"

What on earth did that mean?

Before she could reply, he said, "Shall we go inside? They are about to start."

She trod after him, confused.

Alworth had indeed a box, from which one had a splendid view not only over the stage but also over the spectators.

Pen forgot their exchange and felt the thrill of excitement rush through her. "Look! How splendid the scenery is on stage. The trees look quite real, don't they? How odd, they are selling oranges in the pit! Those velvet curtains seem to be quite heavy; don't you think?"

Alworth observed her with amusement. "Is this your first time at the opera?"

"Yes." Pen stretched her neck. "Why are those ladies pointing their opera glasses at you?"

"I rather think they are inspecting you, my dashing youth."

Pen shook her head. "They are most definitely ogling you." Something occurred to her. "Are you a very sought-after bachelor?"

He barked a laugh. "Heaven help me if I am. But quiet, now."

For the next several hours, Pen dove into a dreamland of music, magic and beauty. Then her mind wandered to Marcus. She'd always thought her first visit to the opera would be with him. Instead, she was sitting next to someone she didn't even know a week ago. Pen squinted at Alworth from the side. He had a nice, classical profile, a proud nose and a stubborn chin. Lips that quirked upwards at the corner, either in a self-conscious smirk or a captivating smile. Everything about him was captivating. All the ladies here seemed to think so. Pen shifted in her seat as she remembered the unpleasant pang she felt when they batted their eyelashes at him.

It had almost felt like… jealousy. But no, that was nonsense, of course. Why would she feel jealous of a man she hardly knew? That would imply she cared about him, but she was certain she did not. They were not friends, not really, not even if he suggested they were.

It took much more to win Pen's loyalty and friendship

than to offer her his carriage, or their clothes, or to invite them for an Indian dessert, or to help them gain membership into White's... she shifted uncomfortably. The truth was, he'd been nothing but helpful and amiable towards her. She'd thanked him by being churlish.

But friendship was very serious business with Pen. She could count her friends on one hand.

Pen suddenly felt herself gripped by the desire to be wearing her petticoats again. To be sitting next to Alworth not as an awkward youth, but as a young lady to be courted. That was such a novel thought that she almost gasped.

What would it be like? To be one of the ladies Alworth admired. What if ... she was to sit there with her finest dress, a fan and gloves... and he was to flirt with her?

Flirt? Bah. Did she have maggots in her brains? She did not want to be courted, and she certainly did not want to flirt!

"So. Did you enjoy yourself, Pen?" Alworth stared down at her quizzically.

Pen blinked and looked around, surprised.

The music had stopped, the curtains dropped, and the spectators were getting out of their seats.

"It is the interval now. A glass of champagne? It is rather hot and stuffy here. Let us stretch our legs outside."

Pen followed him, where a crush of people filled the hallways and the foyer.

"Wait here, I'll obtain some refreshments." Alworth worked himself through the crowd, greeting people to the right and the left.

It was all very lovely here, and the opera was fascinating, the singing fantastic. She hadn't known it was possible to sing like that, but all the people—there were too many people. The smell of sweat and perfume and alcohol made her dizzy.

She leaned against a marble statue.

"Did you see? I could hardly believe my eyes. Rochford is here tonight. Faugh. Such bad *ton*," said a male's voice.

"After what he did to the poor woman last week, it is veritably shocking that he dares to show his face here tonight."

"He is a duke, my dear. He can do whatever he wants."

"If he weren't such a terrible rake, I would consider him for one of my daughters, but, alas—"

"You cannot be serious, Belinda. You'd marry one of your daughters to one as he? I pity the woman he marries."

"You may be right. It is not something any mother ought to do to any of her children. But who else is there?"

"How about Viscount Alworth? Good *ton*, good name, excellent breeding. Used to be engaged to someone, wasn't he?"

"Was he? As far as I know, he's been a bachelor forever. What happened to her?"

"No one knows. It seems the lady let up the engagement. Can you believe that! With one as Alworth on the hooks, how can one leave him for a mere baronet?"

"He is such perfect marriageable material, indeed, but alas, is to leave for India in several weeks' time. I cannot, for the life of me, have one of my children live in India."

"Who is the boy with Alworth?" she heard a woman say on the other side of the statue. "He looks foreign."

"A mystery, my lady, a mystery. But I have it on the best of accounts that it is someone whose identity ought not be revealed," the oily voice of a man replied.

"My dear Hensington. Do say. Who is it?"

The man lowered his voice. "Rumours have it he could be Indian royalty."

"Oh! You don't say! How exciting!"

"Says the doorman at White's. Don't cite me for it."

"Do you think you can get us an introduction, Hensington? For myself and my three daughters…"

"My dear Lady Billingstone, didn't you just say that you can't bear to see any of your children live in India?"

"Yes. But royalty! That does make a difference. Where is Alworth? You must introduce us at once."

"My dear lady. I barely know the man…"

Pen snorted. If Lady Billingstone had high hopes of marrying off one of her three daughters to Indian royalty, she was about to be sorely disappointed.

And Alworth! He was engaged, once? What had happened?

Where was he anyhow? It took him a good time to fetch the refreshments. Her glance went over the crowd and froze.

There.

A tousled black head that stood out above all others.

Her heart started to hammer.

She pushed herself away from the marble statue. The head turned sideways, and she saw his profile. The prominent forehead. That classical nose. She'd recognise it anywhere.

Pen gasped.

"Marcus!" Her voice was shrill, but in the general hubbub of the crowd, it drowned completely.

She fought herself through the crowd. Where was he? Where had he gone?

But Marcus had disappeared into thin air.

"I KNOW IT WAS HIM! I'D RECOGNISE HIM ANYWHERE. I KNOW it, I just know it!"

Pen was hoarse with excitement. She rubbed her moist palms on the velvet seat covers of the carriage as she strained her neck to look outside the window, to see whether Marcus just happened to saunter by on the street.

"Calm yourself, Pen. You yourself just said that when you tried to go after him, he'd disappeared. He may have looked like your guardian from a distance, but likely he wasn't. A trick of the eye."

"I tell you, I am not mistaken. Never about Marcus."

He threw her a probing look. "You seem uncommonly fond of your guardian."

"He is—everything to me."

"Lucky Marcus."

His voice came from a dark corner of the carriage. Pen couldn't see his face to discern whether he was being sarcastic.

The clattering of the hooves stopped as the carriage drew to a halt in front of Pen's lodgings. "Oh. We're here."

In her excitement, when Alworth had asked her where she lived, she'd given him her direction, forgetting entirely that she did not want him to know where she lived.

Pen tore the carriage door open.

Alworth grabbed her by the arm. "Pen. Look at me."

She met his eyes.

"Promise me you won't go running back to the theatre, searching for Marcus."

Pen hesitated. She'd been wanting to do precisely that.

"You know it would be an entirely nonsensical thing to do. If, indeed, it was him, he's long gone by now. It is dark. You'd be unprotected. And, no, don't give me that talk about having a pistol and being able to shoot." He smiled vaguely.

Pen dropped her head. He was right. She nodded. "Very well. I won't."

Alworth looked at her for a moment longer.

"What is it?" Pen whispered.

He loosened his grip on her arm. "Have a good night's sleep. Tomorrow is a big day."

That blasted duel! She'd all but forgotten about it.

"Thank you for a wonderful evening, my lord. It was beyond my wildest imaginings. In fact, it was even better. I will never forget such sublime music."

"I am glad to have been of service," Alworth said, but Pen had already disappeared into the darkness.

CHAPTER 8

*P*en was sleeping, her head dug into her pillow, and she dreamt of Alworth. Even in her sleep, she was irked. She wanted to dream of Marcus. Instead, here was Alworth. The sun glinted in his blond hair, and he smiled in a way that turned her insides into jelly. He bent down and kissed her, and even though it was a dream kiss, she felt a mix of contradictory emotions. She was elated on one hand, on the other outraged. How dare he? And for that matter, how dare she? She'd vowed she'd only ever kiss one man, and that was not Alworth. So how dare he kiss her, even in a dream? *But dear me, he kissed so well.* So she allowed it to go on.

Until someone knocked on the door.

Pen tangled herself up in her sheets and crashed on the hard floor.

Another rap on her door.

"Who is it?" Her voice was thick with sleep.

"Alworth."

Sweet heavens. What was he doing here? Had he just materialised from her dreams? She looked around, panicked.

She wore her nightshirt, and her clothes were sprinkled all over the floor.

"I—uh. I am sleeping!" She pulled on her trousers and hopped around on one leg.

"Open up, Pen."

"I'm not even dressed, yet."

"Tell your valet to hurry."

"I don't have a valet," she muttered.

"Eh? I thought I heard you say you don't have a valet. Say, Pen, can you open the door? Deuced uncomfortable to be conversing with you through this wood. 'Tis not the most salubrious of hallways, either. I think I just saw a rodent flit down the corridor."

She'd bandaged her breasts hastily and dragged a shirt over her head. Stuffing it into her trousers, she padded barefoot over the door, kicking random items of clothing under the bed. Her room was a disaster, but there was Alworth waiting outside.

He'd think it odd if she didn't open. She couldn't just let him stand out there, either.

After dragging her hand through her hair once, twice, she decided it would do. She opened the door.

Alworth had his knuckles raised for another knock. "Ah. Here you are." He let his eyes drift over the room and lifted an eyebrow. "Your valet?"

"Don't have one. I'm ready. Let's go." Pen hopped on one leg as she attempted to pull on a boot on the other.

But Alworth was in no hurry. He stepped into the room and closed the door.

"But my dear, dear boy." He pinched his nose with forefinger and thumb. "There are no words. This is a hovel." He lifted the dingy curtains with his cane to reveal dirt-smeared window panes. "Couldn't you have procured better—and cleaner—lodgings in the Albany, mayhap?"

"No. Anyway, it's none of your—"

"—business," they finished together.

He tapped his cane on the floor and frowned. "I find it extraordinarily irresponsible of your guardian to have left you to your devices like this. Especially if he was present at the opera last night." He shook his head. "Are you still in the frame of mind that it was him?"

Pen nodded. "Most definitely. I would recognise him anywhere."

"So you've said," he murmured. "And yet, given your–shall we say–affection for him—he seems inordinately, if not inexcusably, absent."

Pen sat down on her rumpled bed unhappily. "I know," she whispered.

"Let us approach this matter factually. Based on what evidence are you even certain he is in London? Surely you must have something, anything, some sort of communication, a missive that would indicate his whereabouts?"

Pen hung her head. "He doesn't like to write. But—" her head snapped up. She got up and pulled out a folded missive from a drawer. "I have this."

Alworth held out his hand.

Pen hesitated. This was the only letter she ever had from Marcus. It was infinitely precious to her. She relinquished it with reluctance.

It was a brief note. Pen had memorised it.

Your guardian expressly wishes for you to remain at the Seminary until further notice.

P.P. E.W.

Alworth's eyebrows nearly disappeared under the hairline. "P.P. E.W? Pippin Paul Edgar Williams?"

"*Pro Procurationem*, or on behalf of. E.W. Could be anyone.

Even Edgar Williams. I assume it's a secretary. Or a lawyer."
She shrugged.

"What seminary?"

Pen's mind raced. She could hardly tell him about Miss Hilversham's Seminary for Young Ladies and that fateful night when they were caught sneaking out to the wishing well, and she ended up falling in. The consequence was that Miss Hilversham had written to her guardian about the incident. It had been the address at Bird Street, and Marcus must've still lived there, then. The only response she'd received was this missive signed by E.W.

"The seminary is the boarding school I attended. In Bath."

The envelope had the stamp of the general post office in London. He folded the letter again and stared at the red wax seal. It was barely decipherable. He went to the window to see it closer in the light.

"May I have this letter?"

"Certainly not!" Pen held out her hand to demand it back.

"I would only need it to investigate something. I believe I can help you discover the identity of E.W."

"How?"

"I have my means. Trust me?" He looked at her unwaveringly.

Pen rubbed her neck. "You will return the letter soon?"

"Latest by tomorrow." He pocketed it. "I will return it unharmed, I promise."

Pen nodded.

"Well, then—what on earth are you doing?" He stared at her, aghast.

"Putting on my neckcloth."

"My dear child. This will not do. This will not do at all." He held out his hand and with a sigh, she dropped the crumpled neckcloth into his palm. "I cannot be seen with you in this shocking attire."

He stood in front of her, closer than she felt comfortable, and proceeded to deftly wrap the cloth around her neck. She felt his body heat and smelled starch and cologne. Remembering the dream she'd had, she flushed.

"There." Alworth patted her shoulder. "That is better. You really should acquire a valet."

"It's a matter of funds."

Alworth nodded. "Understandable. Let us go."

THE MORNING FOG HUNG BETWEEN THE TREES.

Pen shivered.

Another group of men appeared promptly. Pen immediately discerned the bulky figure of Blackstone. There was his Second and a man in plain brown clothing, who she assumed to be the surgeon.

"Fine day to duel," Alworth greeted them.

"You are in a terribly chipper mood considering the fact that I might be dead within the hour," Pen grumbled. "Not that I intend to die. But blood will be drawn, for sure."

"Never fear, my friend." Alworth clapped his hand between her shoulder blades, tripping her forward.

"Would you stop doing that!" She swore.

He laughed.

Blackstone's group threw an irritated look at them. Did Pen imagine it, or did Blackstone stare at Alworth? She saw him converse with his man in an agitated manner.

"Chin up, whelp. They're coming over." He turned quickly to Pen. "You have to trust me in this. Let me talk and keep your mouth shut."

"Alworth! It is you." Blackstone shifted his eyes uneasily between her and Alworth. "What is your role here?"

"I am Mr Kumari's Second, of course."

Blackstone swore.

"Language, Blackstone."

"He didn't tell me you were his Second."

"Mr Kumari and I are good friends. Aren't we?" Alworth got out the pistol and polished it. "So naturally, I would be his Second. Especially since I have also taught him the art of shooting."

Blackstone paled. "He was your student? You taught him how to shoot?"

Alworth affirmed.

"You, yourself personally?"

"I loathe to repeat myself. But yes. We have daily shooting lessons. My friend here has become quite adept. Almost as good as me. But not quite." Alworth flashed his teeth.

"For how long?" Blackstone pressed.

"A while."

"I did not know—he never mentioned—that is an entirely different matter, then—" he blustered. Pearls of sweat appeared on his forehead.

"My dear Blackstone. Am I hearing a certain recalcitrance in wanting to go ahead with this duel?"

Pen protested, but Alworth clamped an iron hand on her arm and threw her a quelling glance. She snapped her mouth shut.

Blackstone, too, opened and closed his mouth like a fish. "I—he—that is—"

"Speak up, man. Would you, perchance, prefer to withdraw?"

Blackstone almost melted with relief. "Yes! That's it. Hang honour and all. I withdraw."

"If you will excuse us." Forsyth drew Blackstone aside to consult with him. "Are you certain?" He hissed loudly enough for them to overhear. "The boy doesn't look like he knows his right foot from his left."

"But Alworth does." Blackstone did not even bother to

lower his voice. "If the boy really learned with him, and there is no reason he didn't, you know what that means. He's the best shot in the entire kingdom. And, the boy did say he used to shoot tigers in India. What if it's true? I'm a dead man."

Pen tried with all her might to focus on the foliage of the tree in front of her and pretended not to hear the conversation.

A muscle twitched in Alworth's jaw.

The men returned. "It is as you say," Blackstone's Second said. "We will accept Kumari's apology and—"

"One moment. We never talked about apologies, did we, Pen?" Alworth intervened.

Pen frowned. "No. But then Blackstone also never apologised for having besmirched the Duchess of Ashmore's honour."

"Blackstone?" Alworth's expression was steely.

The man blustered, but eventually he stammered forth an apology.

"In this case, I apologise as well, my lord," Pen said graciously. "For having called you a pig-widgeon. A pasty-faced pig-widgeon, I believe it was."

"No, Pen," Alworth said softly. "I do believe it was corny-faced. Not pasty-faced."

"You may be right. A corny-faced—"

"Apology accepted." Blackstone burst forth. His face was red.

"I believe the matter has been honourably settled," said Forsyth, whose face sagged with disappointment. "Shake hands?"

Blackstone grimaced. Pen stuck out her hand. They shook hands.

Pen wiped her hand unobtrusively on her trousers afterwards.

The men nodded at them and walked away. Blackstone almost ran.

Pen stared after him.

"That was it? All the excitement for nothing?"

"Indeed, it seems somewhat of an anti-climax." Alworth searched his pocket for his snuffbox.

"You knew how he was going to react. You knew from the very first he would never meet me once he saw you." Pen breathed heavily. "You knew he'd withdraw."

Alworth tapped his snuffbox, flicked it open, and took a pinch. "Possibly."

"Best shot in the entire country?" Pen elbowed Alworth. "What is it you forgot to tell me, here? The man almost pissed his pants when he saw you."

Alworth packed up the pistols. "He is a coward. But, yes. I think I'm not such a terrible shot myself."

It occurred to Pen that she'd never seen him shoot. He'd only ever let *her* shoot. He must've known they would back out as soon as they saw his face.

"Thank you," she said gruffly.

"You're welcome, child." He threw her a swift smile. "Let us go eat something. All this excitement makes one positively ravenous."

CHAPTER 9

*A*lworth tossed a newspaper on the dining table. They'd dined lavishly on lamb cutlets, ham and peas, a selection of cheeses, strawberries and Neapolitan cakes. Pen felt she'd never eaten so much. But then they had to celebrate the outcome of the duel.

"Did you know that White's has the entire range of newspapers in the morning room at your disposal? One reads the most interesting things in newspapers, especially old ones." He handed her a glass of sherry. "I dug a bit in the archives the other day—I enjoy reading old newspapers, you know—an entirely useless pastime of mine—and I encountered an interesting story. I am curious about what you think about it."

Pen nipped at the sherry. "Another gossip column?"

"Not entirely. Now listen, closely. It's a story about a Rajasthani princess who'd eloped with an English captain."

Pen, who'd taken too big a gulp from her glass, coughed.

"It was the story of the day. The captain had completely integrated into the Indian way of life. I daresay he must have become Indian himself. What love this must have been." He mused. "What had his name been again? Ray, Reed, Reid, something or other."

Pen's coughing turned to wheezing.

"Apparently, they had a daughter. One wonders what has become of her?" His eyes bore into hers, one eyebrow raised in expectation.

Sweet heavens. He knew.

He knew she was Penelope Shakti Reid, daughter of Adita Kumari, Princess of Bikaner and Captain John Reid.

Not only that, but he also knew that she knew he knew. A tumble of confused thoughts and feelings assailed her. Was her charade over now? Would he openly call her out on it? Would she get thrown out of the club?

She hid her face in the napkin, waiting for the coughing to cease.

"My dear Pen, you ought not to drink alcohol if it does not become you. A glass of water, mayhap?"

"I am fine," she said in a strangled tone.

"What do you think of that story? A fairy tale, is it not?"

She nodded jerkily. "Yes. Undoubtedly. A fairy tale. You ought not to believe everything you read in newspapers."

He lifted one corner of his mouth. "You are entirely correct."

With a whirling mind, Pen disposed of the content of her glass in the plant next to her, not caring whether he saw it, or not. The plant had already started to wilt.

"I daresay you know more about this particular fairy tale. Do you care to tell me the true story?" He'd crossed his legs, pulled out a cheroot and rolled it between his fingers.

Tell him her story? Now? A group of men had just entered, laughing, and started a game of cards by the window.

She licked her dry lips. "I think not," she whispered. She was more shaken than she cared to admit.

He frowned. "After all this, you still will not tell me, will you?"

"I—I am sorry. It's just because—Not now."

"Very well, Pen. Not now." His tone was coolly disapproving.

Would he stop staring at her?

In-between two puffs, he said, "It is an amazing tale, especially if it turns out to be true. Can't help but wonder whether love indeed has the power to make a man give up his entire heritage." He curled his lips in disbelief.

"Ah, yes, you don't believe in love."

It seemed they were to carry on the charade as before. She breathed a sigh of relief. She did not know how to behave in the company of Alworth as a girl dressed as a man. Knowing that he knew her secret, maybe had known for quite some time already, made her feel very self-conscious.

Pen felt like she could not bear it one minute longer in his company. She jumped up. "I will be off now, sir."

She was out the door before he had time to reply.

PEN SPENT THE ENTIRE AFTERNOON SCOURING THE STREETS OF London, in vain, for a sign of Marcus. This couldn't continue. Alworth knew about her masquerade. She was burning through her funds faster than she'd imagined possible, and other than a last-minute averted duel, she had accomplished nothing during her time in London. Her best course of action was to pack up and return to Bath. She would meet Alworth one more time, for she owed him that, to say goodbye.

When the butler admitted her in Cavendish Square with a resigned nod, she was dusty and tired from the long walk.

"Pen. I was about to take a ride in Hyde Park. Join me?" Alworth, impeccably dressed as usual in riding breeches and

Hessians, pulled a primrose from the vase that stood in the foyer and tucked it into his buttonhole.

Pen blinked, bemused. "Why the flower?" she asked.

"Fashion always needs a personal accent, child."

She climbed up into the seat next to Alworth in the curricle, and Alworth flicked the reins.

"May I also try?" Pen asked. Her days in breeches were numbered. Driving a curricle was one experience she'd like to have as a man.

Alworth hesitated.

"I promise not to crash or overturn the curricle."

He gave in. "Very well."

After a quick lesson on how to handle the reins, Pen was thrilled to drive the vehicle through Regent's Park.

"It is such a liberating feeling," she said, and flicked the reins.

"Slow down, this is not a race." Alworth gripped the side.

"I rather like it fast." Pen grinned.

After she'd handed the reins back to him, it occurred to her that he was uncommonly quiet. She cast him a sideways look. He was deep in thought, with a frown on his forehead.

"How much do you really care for this guardian of yours?" he asked abruptly as he drew the vehicle to a halt.

Pen stared ahead in silence.

"I understand your reticence to talk. I myself am not naturally prone to spilling intimate details of my life to people. However, don't you think you owe me an explanation, to say the least?" His eyes bore into hers.

"He's the only family I have left," she whispered.

"Your parents are still in Rajasthan?"

She visibly struggled with herself. "Dead."

"I'm sorry." The sympathetic look on his face made her choke.

It seemed so far away. India. Her childhood. Her parents.

Another world. Another life. Her childhood in Bikaner was a delightful blur of intense colour, the smell of spices, the sound of crickets, the scorching sun on her skin.

There were some things she remembered vividly. She remembered the cloth of her new sari, scarlet interwoven with golden threads. She remembered the cheerful lanterns that lit the courtyard of their villa. The strings of music, the laughter ringing through the night. She remembered her mother's smile as she twirled in her father's arms.

"It was an earthquake."

She heard her voice far away, as she told him in a faltering way what happened that night. There'd been a ball. She remembered how excited she'd been. They'd sent her to bed, because it was late, but she'd crept out of her room and crouched under the mango tree to watch them dance. Her mother, a dark-haired beauty in her golden-cream sari, and her father, handsome and tall in scarlet uniform.

Pen had watched them, jealous, wishing she could dance, too. She remembered Marcus, dashingly handsome in a black evening suit, who'd bowed to her and called her 'princess', with a mocking glint in his eyes, holding out his hand for her very first waltz. She'd danced on clouds.

Then the earth shook, the walls cracked, and all hell had broken loose. A branch crashed down next to her, narrowly missing her, but shielded her from the glass shards and debris that came raining down about her. The walls caved in, right there where they'd been dancing.

"They didn't find me immediately, and I was half-dead myself. It is strange because when you lie there, half in this world, half in the next, you lose all sense of time. I remember little, hardly anything at all. Everything is a blur, a dream. It was almost as if I was watching everything from the outside. As if it happened to a different person."

It was Marcus who'd found her. Marcus, who'd pulled her

out from the debris. But her parents, both, were dead. She'd been orphaned at thirteen. A year later, she was in England, at Miss Hilversham's Seminary for Young Ladies.

"Good heavens, Pen. What an utterly terrible thing to experience when so young. Because of that earthquake, you lost not only your family but also your heritage. It seems you lost your very self." Alworth looked shaken.

"I lost my very self," she echoed numbly. She turned to him with a gasp. "Yes."

Alworth pointed with accurate, eerie knowing to the crux of the matter. She herself hadn't realised it until he said so. She'd lost her childhood. She'd lost her heritage. She'd lost her very self that night. She no longer knew who she truly was.

Pen sat in silence as she digested this.

Was that why she clung to Marcus so much? Because he was her last tie to her childhood in India. To her parents. Because when she was with him, she knew who she was. He was her home. Her rock. A last remnant of her old identity. Without him, she felt like she floundered through life. How could one ever explain this to anyone?

"What about the Maharajah, your grandfather?" Alworth asked.

"Died long before that. Anyway, he'd disinherited my mother when she married my father. I have no family on that side. At least none who'd recognise me."

"Back to your guardian. After he dropped you at that seminary, he just disappeared?"

Pen nodded again.

"When was it the last time you've actually seen him?"

Pen chewed on the inside of her cheeks. "Six years, seven months, three weeks and four days ago."

"Six years!—my dear! How do you know the fellow's even alive?"

She looked at him with wide, frightened eyes. "The letter?" she whispered.

"Ah yes. Which was dated when?"

Pen hung her head. "Also six years ago."

"Look at me, Pen." She met his inquisitive gaze. "Has it ever occurred to you that this Marcus Smith might not be his real name?"

"But why? I've always called him that. Why would he leave me under the misapprehension that this is his real name, if it isn't?"

"That is the question. A fellow might have all sorts of reasons not to want his identity known."

"You make him sound like a criminal. Marcus is the nicest, kindest, most caring person I've ever known."

"Is he?" Alworth gave an odd smile. "Let us hope you're right, child."

"Don't call me 'child'. How dare you insinuate he is anything but the best of characters? You don't even know him. What do you know about loyalty and friendship, anyhow? All you care about is clothes and your club." She curled her hands into hard balls.

"I see you have summed up my character to perfection. Which reminds me I do need a change of linen as the vehicle has whirled up quite a bit of dust. Now. Shall we return? It seems this afternoon's ride is over."

He drove her back in silence. Pen crossed her arms, sulking, all the time knowing she'd been inexcusably rude to him. But he had put to words some of her worst fears, and she dared not think about its implications. No. He must be entirely wrong. Marcus was Marcus. He wasn't a criminal. She knew he wasn't.

Alworth dropped her off at her inn.

Pen did not descend immediately. "I am sorry I was rude

to you. I did not mean what I said. It was inexcusable." She hung her head. "I tend to say things I don't mean."

Alworth's lips quirked. "You mean the part about me not knowing anything about loyalty and friendship. You cut me to the quick." He placed a hand over his heart.

Pen flushed. "It was a cruel thing to say. I have a terrible temper." She scrambled off the vehicle.

"So I have noticed." Then he tipped his hat. "Your servant, brat."

He flicked the reins and drove off.

CHAPTER 10

*C*lub life, Pen decided, was decidedly tedious.

It was too full of men.

Gentlemen who drank, bragged, gambled and placed wagers about things as silly as how many flies crashed against the windowpane in the dining room within the duration of the hour. It made her almost wish for petticoats again, and the company of women, tiresome as they could be.

Maybe she was merely out of sorts because Alworth wasn't here. After having waited the entire afternoon, she decided to leave. Just at that moment, Alworth sauntered into the room, twirling his stick.

"Pen. Well met." He lifted a finger to order a glass of Madeira.

"Alworth." Pen nodded curtly.

"Is anything amiss?" He sat down in the chair opposite hers. "You look somewhat pale."

Pen shook her head. "Nothing is amiss. Too much curry, perhaps."

"Ah yes. You like it spicy." Alworth flashed his bright teeth at her.

"Is there anything you'd like to impart? Otherwise, I'd like to go home and rest. It's been a tiresome day." She would finally pack her trunk and write a letter to Lucy.

"Sit down, my boy. We have more matters to discuss." Alworth took his time lighting his cheroot.

"More?" Pen watched him with irritation. "What matters?"

He took a drag once, twice, and exhaled a perfect circle of smoke.

"The matter of the mysterious disappearance of your guardian."

Pen plopped into the chair with a sigh. "He's probably left London. He may be back in India or the West Indies, for all that's worth, and I'm here scrambling around trying to find a needle in the haystack. I'm wasting my time."

"Don't look so crumpled. I have discovered his identity."

Pen shot up. "What?"

He handed her wordlessly the missive she'd lent him.

"And?"

Alworth looked grave. "It almost makes me wish he were in the West Indies. But, alas, he isn't."

"Spit it out, man!"

Alworth leaned forward. "Did it never occur to you to investigate the seal?"

"It's nearly illegible."

"Not entirely. Here." He pointed with one finger to the red wax blob. "The tip is a lion's head, with two swords crossing behind."

Pen squinted at it. "Is it?"

"Most definitely. My secretary researched it and discovered whose seal consists of such a coat of arms. There are not many. One, to be precise." He hesitated.

"And?"

"You said his name was Marcus Smith. But no Marcus Smith exists."

Pen nodded. She'd figured out that much. "Go on."

"E.W. are the initials of a Mister Edward White. He is a middle-aged man, with a receding hairline and a paunch of a stomach. In short, a man of no particular consequence."

Pen wanted to protest, but he lifted a hand. "Let me finish. He is not your guardian. As I said, this Edward White is just an average sort of man. What gives him consequence is the man he works for."

Suddenly Pen's heart thudded in her chest. "Who?"

"The Duke of Rochford." Alworth said heavily.

Her mind reeled with confusion. "I don't understand."

"I am afraid to have to tell you that your mysterious guardian, Marcus Smith, seems to be none other than Marcus Downing-Smith, the Duke of Rochford. This seal is certainly his. I'm very sorry, Pen." There was an expression of sympathy in his slate grey eyes.

"It cannot be." She licked her dry lips. "Marcus is no duke! You must be mistaken."

"My dear boy, I wish I were. I wouldn't wish that man to be anyone's guardian. But it would make very much sense. Your guardian was in India at about the same time Rochford was. No one knew he returned with a ward, but it is possible. It is also very likely he'd have wanted to adopt an alias abroad."

"Why?"

"He never told you why he was in India?"

Pen shook her head. "He was a family friend. He was my friend. He was just there. Many men are in India, so why not him, too? He said he worked for the East Indian Company."

Alworth shook his head. "Dished you up a Banbury tale right there. He never had to work in his entire life. Had to leave the country rather quickly, though. After he'd seduced the Earl of Essex's wife and shot him in the, um, er, behind. The scandal was all over the papers. Mind you, he was no duke back then, but the Earl of Fenton."

Pen's mouth fell open. "That was Marcus? I refuse to believe it."

"He's done a lot worse. The string of his misdeeds would fill an entire book. It's not without reason he is called the 'Wicked Duke'."

"No. No. No!" Pen shook her head vehemently. "You must be mistaken!"

Alworth looked at her with something akin to pity. "I am sure it must be a shock to you, but there is no doubt it is him. It also explains why he's had to distance himself from you. In fact, that he did so is a credit to Rochford. He might care for you, after all."

"I don't understand. What do you mean?"

"By keeping himself at a distance, he might be trying to prevent his reputation from besmirching yours. Mind you, this is just conjecture on my part. It would be entirely out of character for him to care about anyone's reputation, his own or others."

Her mind refused to register the significance of his words. This was not true. It was a nightmare! Her beloved Marcus a wicked duke? Impossible.

"You're wrong. I'm certain you're entirely wrong." Her voice sounded flat.

"Pen—"

She backed away. Suddenly, it was all too much. She couldn't bear the solicitous expression in his knowing eyes. It was unbearable.

"Leave me alone." She stormed out of the room, nearly ramming into a gentleman who was about to enter. He jumped back, astonished.

Pen ran blindly down St. James's Street, past people and

carriages. Her steps slowed as she walked to Bird Street and stared at the townhouse where Marcus used to live. It was a simple, ordinary kind of house. Certainly not the abode of an earl or a duke.

It was impossible. It had to be.

But what if it wasn't? What if Alworth was right?

Marcus a duke. A wicked duke.

She felt hysterical laughter well up. She choked it down. The people who passed her by threw her odd looks.

After she'd regained her composure, she concluded that there was only one thing for her to do.

She had to go to the Duke of Rochford's residence to see him herself.

CHAPTER 11

Finding the Duke of Rochford's residence was ridiculously easy. All she had to do was go to Grosvenor Square, where all the aristocrats lived, and ask a chimney sweep which of the houses was Rochford's. The boy pointed to a massive grey mansion at the corner of the square. She walked up to it boldly and tapped the brass knocker against the door.

After an eternity, the door opened.

The butler was long and spindly and looked down his hawkish nose at her. He narrowed his eyes.

Another one of those butlers.

Pen drew herself up. "I would like to see the Duke of Rochford. If you please."

"The duke is not in residence. You may leave a card."

Pen sighed. "I don't have any."

He began to close the door. Her foot jammed in quickly. "If he is not in residence, then where is he?"

"I would not know, sir. Now, if you please. Your foot." He stared pointedly at her dusty boot.

She was well on the way to throwing a full-fledged

tantrum. "Of course, you know. You just don't want to tell me. You have no interest, care, nor heart to discover what might prompt me to enquire about where His Grace might be. No. You just want to get rid of me, like everyone else."

She expected him to slam the door into her face, but oddly enough, he didn't.

"May I ask who you are, sir?"

"My name is Pen Kumari. I just need to see what the duke looks like. If he is the person I think he is, then you will regret for the rest of your life how you've treated me. For I am his ward. If he isn't the person I think he is, then never mind." Suddenly Pen ran out of steam. She wiped her forehead with her sleeve. "Forgive my bad manners, for I am very tired of all this."

The butler studied her for a moment, then he seemed to unbend. "His Grace is tall, has black curly hair and green eyes. Maybe this is of help. Now if you will excuse—"

A sick feeling spread in Pen's stomach. "Tell me. Does he like his tea black, no sugar, no milk? He enjoys spicy food and can eat an entire chilli pepper without a blink. And his favourite treat is Turkish delight."

"Yes, sir. Indeed. You are correct." The butler studied her.

Feeling dizzy, Pen leaned against the balustrade. "It is him, isn't it?" she whispered.

"It appears so, sir. However, one might argue that many gentlemen enjoy well-seasoned food and Turkish delight."

Pen nodded, relieved. "You are right. I would not know for sure he is the person I seek until I actually see him."

"You have to forgive me, but he really is not in residence. He hasn't been in a good while."

"Is he back in India?"

"No. He is in the country, but we do not know where." He hesitated before he added, "He does this. Disappear." He spread his hands as if entirely helpless. "Then, when you least expect it, he suddenly reappears as if nothing has happened."

Pen nodded. "Please. Tell me. When he isn't at home, where do you think he is? You must have some sort of idea. Even if you don't know for certain, where do you think he might be?"

"I really cannot say."

Pen chewed on her fingernail in deep thought. "Is he travelling? If yes, where to?"

"It would be unheard of for any butler to reveal such information." He lowered his voice. "I cannot possibly reveal to anyone that His Grace has a marked preference for Madame Beaumont's, for that would be most indiscreet, indeed."

Pen looked straight into his eyes, which were overhung by bushy eyebrows. She pursed her lips. "Very indiscreet. One learns of that kind of information elsewhere. For example, at the clubs."

"Most definitely, sir, at the clubs."

Pen had to refrain from hugging the butler.

"If he happens to come home, say tonight, or tomorrow, can you please tell him I called? I will await a message from him at Oxford Street." She gave him her direction. "Also, tell him it is urgent."

"Very well, sir."

Pen raced back to White's.

ALWORTH SAT IN THE BOW WINDOW, IN THE PRECISE SPOT where his good friend Beau Brummel used to sit before he fled to France to escape his creditors. He'd been part of Brummel's set and learned much of him. A shame, really, that he'd had to flee the country.

He tapped his finger against his brandy glass. He did not

drink, but merely swirled the light brown liquid round and round and round. Between his brows perched a frown. He found himself, most inexplicably, beset by an activity he'd always thought he was a stranger to: brooding. It wasn't a healthy pastime; he decided. Brooding could easily turn into worry. Worry meant he cared about someone sufficiently to let himself be thus distracted. He shifted uncomfortably in his chair. This was worse than worrying. This was a mix of apprehension, anxiety, and concern. As well as annoyance at himself for feeling all this in the first place.

Worry and concern for that brat, Pen.

He swore and set down the glass. Some of the liquid sloshed onto the table.

What did it matter to him what Pen was up to? She was not his responsibility. So why did he care? That question threw him into confusion. Care. By Jove. He certainly didn't care about Pen?

The last time he'd allowed himself to *care* about a woman, he'd had his poor heart thoroughly smashed into a thousand little shards. Crushed, pulverised, and blown away by the wind. There, where his heart was supposed to be, was an organ that pumped blood through his body, but that was about it. Ever since Serena, he was incapable of care. Of being attached to anyone other than himself. Of love. His lips thinned into a sneer. He hadn't felt his heart stir at all in the last decade or so, and he'd been content with that.

Serena. His childhood love. He listened deeply into his heart and found with relief there wasn't so much as a hollow thump when he thought of her. There used to be a time when the mere mentioning of her name caused lightning bolts of agony to shoot through his being. All because he used to believe in love. How young and green he'd been.

He and Serena were going to get married. Granted, they were only children when they'd promised each other eternal love. But by the time he was eighteen, and he stood up with her in the ballroom at his father's country house, he knew it wasn't just a passing fancy. She was the love of his life. She looked radiant and lovely, a diamond of the first water, sought after by many men. How proud he was that she'd chosen him!

They were going to elope together. First to Gretna Green, then they would travel the entire world. Europe, Egypt, India, the West Indies.

On his twenty-first birthday, he'd stood under her window, feeling he could conquer the world. He'd climbed up to her balcony like Romeo and wanted to carry her down.

She stood barefoot in her nightgown, pity in her eyes. "But, Archie. I cannot come with you. These are children's dreams."

He jerked back as if she'd slapped him. "I love you, Serena. I always have. And I know you love me. You always have."

"Of course, I love you, Archie," she'd replied, taking his hands in hers. "I always have." Relief flushed through him, and he felt giddy. "But not like that."

This is when he fell. Not physically, but existentially. "What do you mean? Not like that?" it broke out of him.

She averted her eyes. "In truth, you are more like a brother to me, Archie. A very, very good friend. But even more a brother." She looked back up with a smile, a dimple on her face. "Anyway, there is another reason I can no longer travel the world with you. You won't believe what happened. I received a marriage proposal. From the baron who has been courting me this past summer. And I accepted. He is a colonel, you know. To tell you the truth," she bent over to him, "he is so dashing in his uniform, I fell a little in love with him already." She tinkered a laugh.

A month later, Serena had married her colonel baron.

His world spun out of control as he fell.

He'd been falling since.

All that, Alworth decided, was deeply buried in the past, dead and gone. He'd learned his lesson well: one was better off without love. So why was he dragging up all those memories as he sat in his favourite club, staring through the window at St. James's Street?

He was no longer the green boy he used to be. He'd transformed himself into the dandy he was today. Worldly wise, cynical and eternally bored.

Live life on the cusp. On the surface. Don't dive deep. Don't depend on others. Don't form any attachments. And, for heaven's sake, don't love. He preferred the superficial veneer not only in the appearance he showed to the world but also in his relationships. He'd broken off any relationship to the female sex as soon as he noticed it threatened to penetrate the light, shallow veil. Friends, family, lovers. Casual, light, and fluffy. If that was not possible, then keep them at a distance. Like his family. Thus, let things be.

This odd friendship with Pen had become more than entertainment, and it bothered him.

He downed his brandy and set the glass down with unnecessary vehemence.

Curse it, it was time to finish this.

He would help her find her bloody guardian and hand her over, dust himself off, and move on with his life. He had to turn back to his more imminent problem, one he had been working on before Pen had hurtled into him full force at Pall Mall. His move to India was one thing. He had bureaucratic matters to tend to, overdue visits to his estates, and one other thing he had been procrastinating about.

Dash it if he hadn't entirely forgotten about it.

He needed to find a wife.

A frivolous, pretty sort of thing that wouldn't make too

many demands on him, bear him an heir or two and leave him well alone.

The daughter of a former diplomat in India, Miss Letty Mountroy, came to mind. Porcelain blue eyes, blonde baby curls, a dainty figure, a vapid smile. He'd only met her once at a dinner party.

She'd do very well.

No, he did not care about Letty. But she would certainly make an exemplary wife. One needed not to care about one's wife, he was certain. One merely had to coexist in a reasonable partnership. Marriage was but a business contract, anyway.

He did not really worry about Pen, he reassured himself.

Besides, she would make a terrible wife.

He nearly shot out of his chair.

The deuce! What was the matter with him that he was even thinking along those lines?

Alworth got up, repressing the memory of Pen's expressive, dark eyes, over-brimming with impish laughter, framed by thick lashes. He sensed they veiled a deep sadness, a deep wariness, a deep hurt in her soul. She had lost herself in an earthquake in India long ago. Why was it he had the feeling he understood her more than she did herself?

Stuff and nonsense.

Disturbed, Alworth left the club.

He really had no time to lose.

He should court Letty Mountroy in earnest before Pen led him astray.

CHAPTER 12

*O*nce more, Pen hurtled into him full force in front of the club. She rushed up the stairs just at the moment he emerged from the door. This time, Alworth had the presence of mind to grab the rail by the stairs to counter the impact, so he did not come crashing down.

"Oof," Pen grunted.

"Must you insist on this manner of meeting?" Alworth complained.

"I know where he is," she said breathlessly.

"Indeed?"

"Yes. I went to his residence and asked where he was."

"Did you, now?" Alworth studied Pen. "Let me guess. Likely he is spending his time at various gaming hells, or other houses of ill repute, or worse."

"He's at Madame Beaumont's."

"It is definitely worse."

"Who is Madame Beaumont?" Pen fell into step next to him as they walked along St. James's Street.

"My infant, this is someone whose acquaintance you should be glad you have not made. But it is precisely the kind of acquaintance the Duke of Rochford prefers over everyone else's."

"But who is she?" Pen pressed.

"She is a, er, shall we say, certain lady of repute who runs a certain house of certain repute."

"You are not making any sense at all," Pen complained. "Speak clearly."

"She's a Covent Garden nun."

Pen stopped in the street and stared at Alworth. "She's a nun?"

"She is more of an abbess."

Pen scratched her head. "Why is Rochford staying in the cloister?"

Alworth chuckled. "You misunderstand. The lady runs a vaulting school."

"A school? Like Miss Hilversham's Seminary for Young Ladies?"

Alworth broke into laughter and took some time to recover. "Not quite," he managed to say, eventually. "It's more of a... seraglio."

Pen shook her head. "A sultan's palace in the Orient? Like in the Mozart opera?"

Alworth dried his eyes. "A bordello. A brothel."

Pen's mouth formed a round 'o'. "Why didn't you just say so? All these strange terms."

"It's a delicate matter."

Pen thought. "It can't be Marcus, then. He'd never set foot in a brothel."

"This Marcus seems to be a veritable specimen of morality and proper conduct. I cannot wait to meet him," Alworth said with a satiric undertone.

Pen nodded enthusiastically. "You should. I am certain you two would get along famously."

Alworth muttered something under his breath that

sounded suspiciously like, "devil take him," but she wasn't sure.

Turning to Pen, he asked, "Where are we going, now?"

"To Covent Garden. To that woman's nunnery."

"The deuce you will. Absolutely, utterly, completely, no." Alworth stopped in the middle of the street so that the person behind him ran smack into him.

Pen shrugged. "Fine. You don't have to come. I will go on my own."

She stepped onto the street to cross it. Alworth grabbed her by the arm and pulled her back. "You cannot possibly mean that."

Pen tore her arm from his grip. "Let me go. And I do mean it. It's the only way for me to see Rochford."

Alworth frowned. "Why don't you wait until His Grace returns and call on him like any other reasonably minded person? Leave him a missive, by Jove's beard."

"Because I'm not a reasonably minded person."

"The understatement of the century."

"Besides, I already did that. We don't know when he is returning. Says the butler. I will grow old sitting in my room waiting for a message from him. Marcus doesn't answer letters." Pen strode swiftly down the road. "All I need is a glimpse of the man. If it's not him, I will give up this search and return to Miss H—" she stopped and continued, "I mean, I will return to where I came from."

"Ah, yes, the eternal mystery of the origins of Pen Kumari," murmured Alworth. "Nonetheless, it won't do."

To his surprise, Pen relented. "Very well, if you say so." She trotted next to him, meek and biddable as a baby chick following her mother hen.

Alworth shot her a surprised look. "Good."

"Where are we going now?"

"I thought a new set of boots for you are in order."

Pen sighed. "Very well."

"Hoby's is this way." Alworth pointed with his stick the other direction.

THEY SPENT THE ENTIRE AFTERNOON TRYING ON BOOTS, AND Pen found herself surprised at how much she enjoyed it. Alworth, no doubt, was one of Hoby's best customers.

Alworth, however, seemed oddly preoccupied that afternoon. There was a strain around his eyes and a line around his mouth that never quite seemed to turn up into his usual charming, easy-going smile.

Pen peeped at him uneasily. "You seem in a peckish mood today?"

They had ordered three pairs of boots each and had them delivered to Alworth's home. Alworth did not trust that they would be safe in Pen's inn. She was to pick up the parcel from Cavendish Square later. Then Alworth took her to Gunter's for ices, and Pen was certain she'd never enjoyed herself more.

"Hm? What do you mean?"

"It's almost as if you're brooding. You're not worried about anything?" Pen popped a spoonful of pistachio ice into her mouth.

"Worried!" He sat up straight. "By George. No!"

"Then what is the matter?"

Alworth folded his arms and frowned. "Nothing is. I am to be married, that's all."

Pen's spoon fell onto the table. "Oh! I had no idea."

"That is, not quite so imminently." The frown line between his brows grew thicker. "That is, maybe it is rather imminent, if you consider I am to leave for India in two months' time. I'd like to take my wife along then."

Pen snapped her mouth shut. "Who is she?"

"Miss Letty Mountroy."

Pen decided on the spot that she hated Miss Letty Mountroy. She dragged up every inch of politeness from the depths of her being. "Then I congratulate you. Lucky Miss Mountroy."

Alworth stirred moodily in his ice cream. "Hm. Yes. She doesn't know I am going to marry her."

Pen stared. "Heavens, she doesn't know?"

"I haven't proposed yet." Alworth scratched his cheek. "I ought to talk to her father first."

"I gather the custom is to let the lady know that one intends to marry her." Pen propped her head on her hand. "Before that, one might also want to talk to her to see whether one actually likes her. Considering the fact that one is to spend the rest of one's life with her."

"It does seem like the thing to do." Alworth frowned into his ice goblet.

"You don't seem particularly enthusiastic about the prospect," Pen observed. She felt something lighten inside, something like relief.

A smile flitted over his face. "Pray, what man is enthusiastic about getting shackled? And you are quite right, I am not enthusiastic. She probably isn't either, which is excellent. Precisely what I want."

Pen shook her head. "You're not making any sense, Alworth. Why is this excellent?"

"It is but a business transaction," he explained. "Therefore, it is quite good that there are no feelings involved. I like things that are simple and to the point."

Pen was aghast. Surely, he could not mean this? She saw Alworth in an entirely new light. "What about love?" she burst forth. "How can you marry someone you don't love?"

"Love?" A sardonic look passed over his face. "We are back at that topic, are we? I can do without it."

"But, why?" Pen had forgotten about her ice, which was melting into a green soup.

"Nothing ever comes of it."

"But to be married for life to a person you don't even care for! That's a terrible sort of fate."

"My dear Pen. You are not, at heart, a romantic, are you?" He seemed to remember something. "But of course you are." He pursed his lips as he studied her. "You grew up with that legendary love story."

"I have no idea what you're talking about." Pen dedicated her entire attention to shovelling the melted ice into her mouth.

"Your parents."

He was right. Her father, the British officer, her mother, the Indian princess. An impossibility. So, they eloped. They lived happily ever after, until Pen came along, who always seemed to be in the way, somehow. She was raised by Ayah, whom she adored.

Pen did not know that her face reflected her emotions like a mirror.

"Tell me. Were they actually happy, your parents?" Alworth seemed to enjoy studying her face.

Pen thought. Fact was that she'd seen very little of them. "Of course they were. At least, I think they were."

Her mother had been ethereally beautiful. Her father dashing and handsome. She discovered to her horror that she could no longer recall their faces. Whereas she could remember her kitten Snowball very well. He'd been entirely black, with one white paw.

"Why do you not want to love your wife?" she pursued, not understanding why this bothered her so much.

She saw a look of discomfort flit over his face.

He pulled on his cravat as if it were too tight. "Emotions

tend to complicate life. I prefer life to be uncomplicated and light."

Pen digested that. It was contrary to her entire nature. She felt everything deeply. A life, a relationship without feelings, was impossible. She decided she did not really know Alworth very well if that was what he really believed in. A feeling of disappointment sank to the pit of her stomach, where it churned and fermented. Then her head snapped up.

"I am certain I love Marcus," she informed him. Then she gasped and clasped her hand over her mouth.

Alworth's eyes widened, then filled to the brim with a devilish light. "Do you, my boy?"

A hot wave flushed over her, and she wanted to disappear into the ground.

"I mean, not in that manner. Not as you think…" Her voice petered out.

He threw his head back and burst into a guffaw of laughter that shook his entire body. Pen glanced around nervously. They were attracting attention.

"Pen. Oh, Pen. You are a joy to be with. I swear I haven't laughed in this manner since—" He burst into a peal of laughter again. "I can't even remember when I've last laughed like that." He wiped his eyes. Then he laughed again.

Pen sat straight and stiff. "I fail to see what's so funny, sir."

Alworth slapped her on the shoulder so that her nose dipped into her melted green pistachio soup. "Pen, my boy. The look on your face is priceless. It is none of my business whom you love. Even if it is your guardian who turns out to be a lecherous old duke."

With a grin, he pulled out a handkerchief and handed it to her. Pen wiped her nose.

"He's definitely not a lecherous old duke," she muttered.

For sure he wasn't. He couldn't be. But suddenly she

wasn't so certain anymore. What if he was? What would she do then?

Pen shifted uncomfortably in her chair and swallowed. Alworth certainly had regained his old self. He led her out of the coffeehouse, twirling his stick.

"I will leave you here, my cub. Take my carriage and go home. I have business to attend to nearby. I need to make a call on Mountroy." He quirked an eyebrow at her. "Unless you'd like to accompany me?"

What. And watch him court Letty Mountroy? She'd rather face Blackstone in a duel, fists only.

"No, thank you," Pen said hastily. "I have business myself to conduct."

Alworth nodded at her and strode down the street.

Pen looked after him, feeling for one moment that she wanted to run after him and talk him out of his crazy plan.

Then she pulled herself up.

It was none of her business whom he married, whether or not he loved his bride. Miss Letty Mountroy. Bah. He should marry this Letty Mountroy and go to India and live happily ever after, and she would marry Marcus and live happily ever after.

Speaking of Marcus.

Madame Beaumont was waiting.

CHAPTER 13

*M*adame Beaumont's did not look at all like a house of ill repute. It was an ordinary grey house with white windows and a pale green door framed by two white colonnades.

Pen stood in front of the door for several minutes, shifting from one foot to another. She lifted her hand to knock, then dropped it again. Taking a deep breath, she tried to summon up all her courage. This wasn't easy. She swallowed and raised her hand once.

Someone grabbed her arm from behind with an iron grip and pulled her back.

"So this is what you're up to when I'm not looking," a voice hissed into her ear.

"Let me go!" She kicked him in his shins.

"Dash it, Pen, was that necessary?" Alworth rubbed his knee with his free hand.

"Why are you following me?" She scowled at him to cover her relief that he was here.

"I noticed that instead of going to your home, the carriage took a different turn, and so I decided to follow you."

She writhed in his grasp. "Stop following me."

"This is what you've been planning all along, haven't you? I can't let you for a minute out of my sight." A muscle flicked angrily at his jaw.

"This is none of your business. Let go!"

Alworth seemed to battle with himself. Then he released his grip on her. "Very well. We will proceed as follows. I will go inside and ask for the Duke of Rochford. You will wait outside."

Pen rubbed her arm. "No. You will wait outside, and I will go in. I am, after all, the one who has to recognise him, not you."

"By Jupiter, Pen, I have better things to do than stand outside in front of a bloody bawdy house and argue with you." His mouth was tight and grim. "You will not set a foot inside the house and that is final."

She poked her finger into his waistcoat. "You're neither my father nor my guardian! You don't decide what I do."

"No, thankfully I am not. But on my honour as a gentleman, I cannot let you set foot in this house. You know very well why. Do not challenge me in this matter, or we shall call this charade of yours over, once and for all." His voice had turned deadly cold, his eyes slits of steel.

Pen shivered. Who would've known that Alworth turned frightfully intimidating when angry?

"They will eat you like trifle for dessert," he added more mildly. "Then I have to go anyway to rescue you. I don't relish that thought."

Pen struggled with herself. Her reasonable half knew he was right. She had no business being here. But her stubborn self wouldn't give in so easily.

"Penelope Reid."

She gasped. Her eyes shot up to meet his. A fire burned in his depths.

"Would you consider me your friend?" There was something in his face, as though her answer mattered to him.

"I trust my friends with my life," Pen hedged.

"In other words, no." Alworth sighed. "What, ye gods, would it take to get accepted into the Almighty Pen's circle of friendship and trust?" He tapped his stick on the ground. "For it comes down to that, whelp. You will simply have to trust me. I will go in there and ask for your duke's whereabouts."

"And then?"

"If he is indeed there, I will do my utmost to persuade him—" he pulled a grimace as if the thought was distasteful to him, "to leave his pastime and come outside. So you can identify him. It will be a bit of work. Not to say, the Abbess might disapprove."

"In which case it might simply be easier for me to go in to begin with—" Pen started anew.

"The matter is settled." Alworth pushed Pen aside and knocked on the door.

It opened on the second knock, and a maid with a peaked face looked out. She assessed them with one glance. "Come in, sirs."

Alworth threw Pen a meaningful look and stepped across the threshold.

The door closed in her face.

Pen walked over to the birch tree in front of the house and leaned against it, watching the door. She had to admit; she was relieved she didn't have to enter that house. But would Alworth really look for the duke there? Could she really trust him?

She picked a piece of bark from the tree and chewed on it. She'd observed a stable boy do it once. It looked nonchalant, so she did the same. It tasted bitter. Pen spat it out.

Alworth was growing more and more of a mystery to her.

At first, she'd thought he was a mere dandy. He insisted he lived the life of the superficial. Then why his solicitousness regarding her safety? Why his insistence on friendship? It seemed contradictory. Her feelings were contradictory, too. The pang of disappointment when he'd said he did not believe in love had surprised her. The feeling of shock when he'd announced he'd get married. Pen rubbed her forehead. What was she doing, thinking about Alworth, when she was supposed to be thinking about Marcus?

At that moment, the door opened, and Alworth stepped out. Barely ten minutes had passed.

She rushed up to him. "Is he there?"

Alworth shook himself, as if ridding himself of something distasteful. "No. He's long gone."

Her shoulders slumped. "What happened?"

"Madame Beaumont herself greeted me. She would not immediately tell me whether the duke was here. She was rather reticent, talked about protecting her customers, etcetera, etcetera. Then someone called for her, and she left me for several minutes. In the meantime, the peaky-looking girl who opened the door came into the room to serve drinks. It took her only a minute to tell me all about the duke —after I'd given her a bribe."

"You bribed her! How clever of you."

"The duke indeed had been here for the last several days. He's a permanent customer, as good as living there. But with your kind of luck, he left shortly before we arrived."

Pen looked at him in disbelief. "You're roasting me."

He lifted an eyebrow. "My dear Pen, why would I do that?"

Indeed. Why?

"I thought we'd established that you simply had to trust me in the matter. It turns out the duke took his, er, lady to a ridotto at Vauxhall gardens."

Pen's face brightened. She'd been with Marcus to Vauxhall once and enjoyed herself tremendously. There'd been concerts under the night sky, dancing, and fireworks.

"Let us go there right away." She pulled Alworth to the carriage.

He groaned.

VAUXHALL WAS EVERYTHING IT PROMISED TO BE. IT WAS A pleasure garden accessible by boat. There were dancers and tightrope walkers, and a balloon that had begun to ascend. Strains of Handel hung in the air. In the centre was a Chinese pavilion, and beyond were the secret alleys and walks for amorous adventures, for which Vauxhall was so famous. Lampions hung between the trees, which would be lit by dusk.

Pen looked around, fascinated, her eyes sparkling saucers, her mouth pursed to an astonished O. She'd forgotten how magical the place was.

"Enjoying yourself?" Alworth watched her with amusement.

"What is that?" Pen pointed at a construct behind the orchestra.

"That is the Turkish tent. Shall we look at it?"

Alworth strolled over. It was supported by eight columns and was lavishly decorated with flowers and feathers. From its dome hung crystal chandeliers.

"I haven't seen this before." Pen marvelled at the structure. "At least, I don't remember it."

A party of people dined inside. A portly, well-dressed gentleman turned toward them and raised his quizzing glass. "Alworth! Well met. What good chance that you happen to pass by. Join us? Your friend as well, of course." He nodded at Pen.

"Lord Mountroy," Alworth introduced. "This is Pen Kumari."

Pen gave a quick bow.

"Ah yes. I have heard of you. You hail from India? I myself have resided there for the past decade or so. Terribly hot, the weather. Not to mention the food. Alworth here won't let that deter him. He is to take the passage himself soon, aren't you?"

"Indeed. I daresay I am in the process of training my palate to the spiciness of that country's food." He grinned at Pen.

"All this talk about hot spicy food makes me thirsty. There, take a drink." Lord Mountroy lifted a finger, and a footman appeared with a tray of champagne glasses. "You will have to excuse me, gentlemen, as I see Lady Mountroy summoning me. Let us talk later about your plans." He nodded at Alworth and returned to his wife.

Alworth took a glass of champagne and handed it to Pen.

A slim figure separated from the group and tripped towards them.

"Well, would you have it," Alworth raised his glass. "Miss Mountroy." He revealed a bright set of teeth and a dimple as he smiled. "Well met."

She wore an excessively plumed bonnet and nodded at him, so that the entire construct wobbled up and down. "La. Viscount Alworth." She fluttered her eyelashes at him.

"Miss Letty Mountroy. This is my good friend, Pen Kumari."

Miss Mountroy's eyes widened. "The Indian Prince? It has come to our ears that you have made an acquaintance with an Indian Prince."

By George. She talked like the king. With a lisp. Pen fidgeted uncomfortably. "Er."

First-rate reply, Pen. Eloquent and sensible. She raked her

mind for something more but was rendered speechless by her violet vapid eyes blinking rapidly. Pen wondered whether she had a dust speck in them.

Alworth threw Pen an amused look. "News travels fast."

"How fascinating," Miss Mountroy breathed.

Letty Mountroy was every bit as birdwitted as Pen feared she'd be. When she talked, she sounded breathless. She looked like a doll, with wide eyes, pale eyebrows and perfect corkscrew curls. Her smile was pasted on her face. Pen watched her closely. Indeed, there was no depth of emotion at all. Pen wondered what Alworth saw in her. Then she remembered that he'd said precisely that her lack of depth was what he found so attractive.

She watched how he bent over her, listening to her lisping account of the balloon ascent.

Then she batted her eyelashes at Pen.

Pen, who just took a sip of her champagne, swallowed the wrong way and spluttered. "I beg your pardon. If you will excuse me." She left the tent to cough up the liquid from her air pipe.

"I have never seen an Indian Prince before," she heard Miss Mountroy tell Alworth. "It is like in a fairy tale, is it not?"

Oh, heavens. How could Alworth bear listening to her?

Pen turned away and watched the crowd. Her gaze was arrested when a well-dressed young man strode across her path. Slim physique, proud head, with a devil-may-care tilt to his chin. Pen dropped the champagne glass. She knew this figure! She'd quarrelled with him daily on the ship. No, it wasn't Marcus. It was— "Fariq!" she bellowed and elbowed her way through the crowd.

Fariq, Marcus's valet. Dressed in an excellently tailored suit, plus a turban and a stately beard. Goodness! Fariq with a beard! The last time she'd seen him, he'd been a lanky boy, several years older than herself. Marcus had plucked him from the streets of Bombay and made him his valet. They'd been rivals for his attention.

He stopped and turned, with a frown knitting his forehead.

"It *is* you! Fariq!" Pen held herself back from hugging him just in time. "I've never been so glad to see someone."

Fariq's mouth dropped. "By the eye of Shiva. Miss Penelope? How can it be? Is that really you? You've grown up. Into a—man?"

She pulled him behind the pavilion. She felt like laughing and crying simultaneously. For where Fariq was, Marcus was not far behind.

"Fariq! I'm so glad to see you!" She finally fell around his neck.

"But, Miss Pen. In such an outfit!" He untangled himself, looked her up and down, and tsked disapprovingly. He himself was dressed in the most exquisite clothes; his boots shined to perfection.

When did Fariq become so noble? She remembered the scrawny, lively youth he'd been on the ship. He'd acquired a perfect King's English and carried himself with pride.

"I take it you're supposed to be a man?" He looked at her critically. "The trousers are too short. Is that a waistcoat? Your boots are passable. Your haircut is a disaster. You'd have been better off wearing a turban."

"I know. I know. It's beside the point. Can we stop talking about what I'm wearing?" He was almost as bad as Alworth. "Where is Marcus?" Pen stretched her neck.

"Marcus? Oh. You don't know."

"Know what?"

"I no longer work for him."

"You don't? But what are you doing now? And where is he?"

"I'm the proud owner of my very own gaming salon, Miss Pen." He puffed up his chest. "I'm very, very successful."

"A gaming salon!"

"The Perpignol's. With His Grace's help, of course. He is my patron."

"Perpignol's! His Grace!" Pen felt a stone sink in her stomach. She remembered Alworth saying Perpignol's was one of the worst gaming hells that only people like the Duke of Rochford frequented.

"So it is true," she whispered. "Marcus is the Duke of Rochford?"

"You didn't know? Oh. You might not. He didn't want anyone to know of his identity while he travelled to India. He was the Earl of Fenton. We always thought of him as Mr Smith, didn't we? Then, as soon as we put our foot on English soil, it turns out he's one of the most powerful dukes in the country." Fariq looked more than satisfied with his lot. "He came into his title shortly after he dropped you off at that school. I continued working for him for a while, but then, there is more to life than dressing a person and sorting his waistcoats. It's damnably boring. Remember how we used to play cards on the ship? There was nothing better to do?"

"We gambled for seashells, and when we ran out of those, we used fishbones. One fishbone worth a shilling. Horrendously high stakes."

Fariq grinned at her. "I remember you cheated most awfully, Miss Pen."

"And I've never seen a worse loser than you. Remember the tantrum you threw when you lost a three-day game against me?"

"Me? Bad loser? Where would you get that idea?" His eyes sparkled with memory. "Ah, life was hard then, but we did have our amusing moments, did we not?"

"It was all thanks to Marcus."

"Aye. I owe him my life. I was a street boy pickpocketing His Grace's pockets when he caught me. And now, look at me! I'm the true king of London." He bent over and whispered, "The people just don't know it yet."

He was right. Fariq sparkled with confidence and success.

"His Grace taught me everything, and I quickly became the best gamester in London. He was most gracious in helping me acquire the locality for my club. It was an overnight success. The games at White's and Brooke's, pah, are paltry. We dip deep. Fortunes are made and lost within the hour. Perpignol's a very exclusive club where admittance is by card, only. People are scrambling over themselves to set their foot inside." He flicked away a speck of dust on his arm sleeve. "And even then, we turn away half of the people who are begging to join."

But Pen didn't listen. She felt wretched. "Marcus is the wicked duke."

"Wicked!" Fariq pushed out his lower lip in contemplation. "I wouldn't exactly call him wicked. But, true, lately he's been playing hard, and he's been looking too deeply into his cups. Can't help but wonder what ails the old man."

"Where is he now?" She searched the crowd.

"I have no idea. Is he here? I am here on another errand."

"Can I find him at Perpignol's, then?"

"If he does play, this is where he is, naturally. Though I haven't seen him for the last few days. He tends to disappear. One simply has to wait until he reappears." Fariq shrugged. The butler had said something similar.

"I've heard all sorts of stories." Pen knit her forehead in worry.

Fariq evaded her eyes. "It's just stories, Miss. But tell me about you."

She gave him a summary of her situation. "What am I to

do? I can't stay at those lodgings forever. And the butler at Grosvenor Square won't let me in."

"No. Old dour face has strict instructions not to let anyone in the house. You are in a pickle, aren't you? I will give Rochford a message when I see him. *If* I see him. It will be taken care of. I promise."

Pen sighed in relief. "Tell him I'm in lodgings in Oxford Street. I await instructions there. After all, he is my guardian."

Fariq nodded. "I will tell him when I see him. Until then, do you need anything, money, perhaps?"

Pen shook her head. "For the time being, I am fine."

"Very well, Miss. But should you need anything, anything at all, the doors of Perpignol's are open to you. Any time." He winked at her, then Pen watched his purple turban disappear in the crowd.

She returned to the Turkish pavilion, her head in a whirl. Alworth waited in front, tapping his stick on the ground impatiently.

"Where have you been?" he growled. "I've been searching high and low for you. In this crowd it is virtually impossible to find anyone."

"It is fine. We can go now." Pen trotted beside him, repressing the turmoil she felt inside.

Alworth shot her a look. "You seem to have an air of excitement about you."

"I found him." It burst forth from her.

Alworth stopped in his tracks. "Rochford?"

"No. Maybe. His valet." Pen dropped her head. "His former valet. You were right that Marcus is Rochford. Fariq confirmed it. He will give him a message from me. If he remembers."

"I'm sorry, brat. You'd have deserved a worthier

guardian." There was a look of sympathy on his face. Pen looked away.

For the first time, she did not rise to Marcus's defence. Something kept her from telling him that Fariq was the owner of Perpignol's. And that she planned to go there.

Alone.

CHAPTER 14

"*I* will be out of town for a while," Alworth imparted to her as they stood in front of the shabby inn where she held her lodgings. "I have some business in Wiltshire."

His estate in Wiltshire was run by a very efficient steward who sent him weekly reports. Alworth's take had been, so far, not to meddle in something that ran very well without his interference. His family, however, interpreted his continual absence as indifference to his legacy.

"You're more interested in your tailors than in the agricultural development of the land," his brother James had once accused him. There was some truth in those words; yet until now, he hadn't felt bothered by them in the least.

Why was it lately that he felt he had to get involved in his steward's affairs and show some interest? And why this sudden urge to visit his brother and sister, Bea and James? In addition to, good heavens, his spinster aunt, Honoria.

He suspected this change in his attitude had something to do with Pen. More than once, the thought crossed his mind that he really wasn't better than Pen's unworthy guardian.

Hadn't he abandoned his family similarly as Rochford had abandoned Pen? The notion left him squirming. Anyway, he ought to visit them before he departed for India. Who knows, he might never see them again after that.

"For how long will you be gone?" Pen asked.

Did he imagine it, or did her tone sound woeful?

"I suppose a fortnight at the minimum." Alworth watched Pen from under hooded eyes.

A shadow flitted over her narrow face. "Very well. I shall miss you," she said gruffly.

He took her by the chin and tilted it up. There was a soft colour in her sweetly curled lips. Her eyelashes swept down as a flush covered her high cheekbones.

He stared, mesmerised, at her gently parted lips.

So tempting. So sweet. An overwhelming desire to kiss her overcame him.

He lowered his head. The smell of honeysuckle entered his nose. Underneath that manly facade, she was all woman. A courageous woman of the likes he'd never known before. A woman worthy of loving.

The deuce! Was he out of his mind?

Alworth dropped his hands and took a step back. All of a sudden, he did not know what to do with them, so he fiddled around with his cravat. "Don't get into any kind of trouble," he said huskily. He cleared his throat. "Like seeking Rochford in some gaming hell. Or getting called out for another duel, or worse."

The blush on her cheeks, which for one moment had intensified to a strong rose, faded. She evaded his eyes. "Nonsense. Why would I do that? I will go to White's every day, eat breakfast, lunch and dinner there, read newspapers and be perfectly bored until you return."

"Sounds like a good plan."

"Well. I will be off, then." Pen seemed oddly reluctant to leave.

He gave her a curt nod and left.

Damnation. What had that been about? Alworth strode down the road to regain his composure. His waistcoat felt too tight and his cravat too constricting. A breath of fresh air would surely do him good.

Alworth pondered on her response as he approached Berkeley Square, twirling his stick. The brat, no doubt, was up to something. At the moment, there was nothing he could do about it. Hadn't he decided not to immerse himself any longer in her problems? She was not his concern. Not his responsibility. Not his ward. Yet... of all people, why Rochford?

He sighed.

Conscience was a damnable thing.

Alworth stopped in front of a dapper townhouse with well-polished iron fencing. Cheerful red begonias decorated the windowsills. This was a friendly house. He hesitated. He could still turn around, pretend he was merely walking past, taking a stroll. He took a big breath, pulled up his shoulders and climbed the stairs to knock on the door. It opened almost immediately. Had they seen him arrive from the window?

"Archie!" He hadn't heard his childhood name in a very long time. He regarded the pretty, dainty brunette with the sparkling eyes, who opened her arms to embrace him.

"Hello, Serena."

CHAPTER 15

he next day, Pen called in Cavendish Square to bid Alworth goodbye but was informed by the indomitable butler that Alworth had left for Wiltshire. Already? She hadn't known that he'd intended to leave so immediately. But of course. A man like him had no time to lose. He had his estate and business affairs to settle. And, no doubt, a family to visit... An odd feeling beset Pen. First Marcus, then Rochford. They all abandoned her, the people in her life.

Pen stopped in the middle of the sidewalk and slapped herself lightly on the cheek. "Stop this nonsense at once, Penelope," she chided herself.

The boy who came towards her threw her a frightened look.

"I'm just talking to myself," Pen explained, and he nodded and scurried away.

Pen had her friends still from the seminary. Even though they were married with their own families and had no time for her. And there was Fariq. The owner of the Perpignol. Pen's heart started to hammer. With Alworth gone to oversee her every move, she would, of course, seek Fariq. Alworth never needed to know.

The Perpignol was located in a red brick house in Pall Mall. She braced herself for trouble with the doorman, after all, she was not a select member of the club. But after she mentioned Fariq's name, he nodded. "Mr Fariq said you might come."

He led her through a set of ordinary looking drawing rooms, then opened an inconspicuous tapestry door. Lights lit the stairs, and she followed them down with a growing sense of curiosity.

The gambling salon was underground. Decorated entirely in scarlet and gold, it looked elaborate, if not decadent. It wasn't as big as she'd expected. There was a roulette table, a faro table and several other tables where people played whist, picquet and vingt-et-un. A hush of concentrated silence engulfed the room. Only the rattle of the ball in the roulette wheel was heard.

There was Fariq, in a dark suit and golden turban, looking stern and formidable as he headed the roulette table. He was, at most, five years older than Pen, yet with that dark beard of his, he looked decades older. Who would've thought he could look so intimidating? He must've seen her enter, yet did not acknowledge her presence.

Pen grabbed a glass of champagne that a footman offered her and strolled through the room. She saw immediately that Marcus was not there. Was it too early, maybe? Would he come later?

A man threw down his set of cards with a sigh and pushed back the chair. His partner, a gentleman in a wine-red coat, who remained seated, studied Pen. "Care to play?" he drawled.

She shrugged. "Why not."

Pen had been taught the tricks of the trade by one of the

most accomplished gamblers. The man who sat across from her seemed to think he could easily fleece her. She bit down a smile.

The game turned quickly, and Pen had the upper hand.

Her opponent threw down the cards. "Hats off, you're not to be underestimated," he admitted grudgingly, as he handed her her winnings. "Another round?"

Pen declined. She stuffed the bills into her pocket and strolled into the next room, where there was a similar scenario. She was in no playing mood. She sat down in an armchair and waited for Marcus.

As soon as she'd settled, a shadow fell over her.

"Well, well, well, look who's here," said an oily voice above her.

Pen looked up, straight into a florid, leering visage.

"Blackstone." Pen took a gulp from her drink. "Still about insulting hapless females?"

"Not me. My taste runs to spanking brazen-faced milk-sops these days." He bared his yellowed teeth.

Pen gripped her glass. She had to be on guard.

"You played foul the other day. Might've mentioned Alworth was your mentor." He waggled a fat finger at her. "With someone like him protecting you, no wonder you tear your insolent mouth wide open. But when he is not about…" His eyes wandered through the room. "Where is he? Is he here?"

Pen's mind raced for an answer.

"Oy. Have you seen Alworth in these rooms?" Blackstone called to a group of men by the fireplace.

Pen recognised with a sinking heart that Forsyth and Pennington were among them.

"He's stepped out for a moment and will be back shortly," she lied.

"Alworth? He's not a member here for all I know," Pennington answered.

"He isn't, is he? This place is too low for the likes of him." Blackstone settled down in a chair opposite hers and leaned up close, so that she could see the little red veins in the white of his eyes. "Listen, whelp. You played foul, and I was forced to back out of the duel."

"Forced? It was your choice." Pen's voice squeaked. "You were too chicken-hearted to face me, that's what."

A vein pulsated in his temple. "I will have my revenge, you know," he hissed, spewing her face with spittle. Pen wiped her cheek. "I insist on another duel. Not with pistols, mind you. But with bare-handed fists." He cracked his knuckles. "Or are you too much of a milksop to meet me with the fists?"

Forsyth and Pennington had gathered around them. "Prime idea, Blackstone. Where shall we do it?"

Pen's heart sank. How was she to get out of this? "Our duel is completed. You backed out and apologised, and that is the end of it. There is no need for a repeat."

"On the contrary, there is every need. A fist fight is excellent. Let us place bets immediately. Did you hear, gentlemen? The fight of the season is about to happen." Forsyth announced to the room in general.

"What, what?" Forsyth's general announcement drew attention.

"Blackstone against Kumari. Who wants to wager?"

Word spread like wildfire, and the room filled with enthusiastic men placing their wagers. Two groups formed immediately, the majority for Blackstone.

Pen broke out in a sweat. Her protests drowned in the general din.

"What is going on here?" Fariq had entered the room.

"The rules say no brawls in these rooms. I will revoke the membership of anyone who starts a brawl."

"Fariq! They want me to fight him in a fistfight." Pen felt nauseous at the mere thought.

"Leave the matter to me," he muttered under his breath.

"Fariq. You're the man we need now. Record it in your books. The match itself will take place in Regent's Park." Forsyth slapped a hand on Fariq's shoulder, whose face remained deadpan. "Surely you will not oppose us placing wagers?"

Fariq held up his hands. "I have another proposal, gentlemen. Why boxing? What is the excitement in that? Flesh punching flesh. No. Let it be what these rooms are for." He pulled out a pack of cards and flipped them from one hand to the other. "Lady Fortuna's favoured pastime: a match of cards."

"Boring." Forsyth pulled a face.

"The fist has more impact," Blackstone slammed his fist against the palm of his hand. "Wouldn't you say?"

"Gentlemen," Fariq lifted back his tailcoats and sat in a chair, crossing his legs. "I represent Mr Kumari. If you agree to this match being one of cards, the stakes will be this." He pulled out a scarlet book, raised a golden quill and scribbled down a number.

Silence settled over the room. Then a general din broke out of men scrambling to place their wagers.

"Very well, man. A duel of cards, it is. At what odds? Let it be good, mind you," Blackstone said.

Pen glanced at Fariq, who lifted a hand with his fingers spread.

She ran her tongue over her cracked lips before saying, "5:1?"

Fariq nodded imperceptibly.

The men muttered. "This is playing deep. If Fariq represents him, he may not be the greenhorn he appears to be."

"Very well." Blackstone grinned evilly. "This, plus Fariq quadrupling the final winnings, should yield a good win. What say you, Fariq?"

"Very well." He was nonchalance in person.

Good heavens. Pen exhaled a shaky breath. Count on Fariq to save the day. A match of cards she could do. Her eyes met his. There was a twinkle in them.

"Thank you," she mouthed.

"Wait!" Blackstone raised an arm for attention. "We have to set a time and place first. When is this duel to take place?"

"Saturday in a fortnight, this location," Fariq decided. "Be punctual."

"Fariq." Pen turned to Fariq with a sigh. "How on earth do you see this happening?"

He'd invited her into a private study that consisted of a walnut desk, several shelves with books, and an oil painting of a tiger hunt in Bengal.

"I do see this happening, indeed." He rubbed his hands. "This is excellent business. Word will get out, and not only will this be very good advertisement for the Perpignol but also good money. Provided you win. Which you shall."

Pen shook her head. She slumped in her chair and rubbed her temples. A throbbing headache had taken over, and she felt exhaustion seep into the very marrow of her bones.

"I have every confidence you will best Blackstone. You always were a natural talent at cards." Fariq sat behind his desk and looked every bit the owner of the club.

"My playing has become very rusty. I had better order my casket," Pen grumbled.

"Nonsense. A drink?" Fariq lifted a bottle.

Pen shook her head. "I had better return home. Don't forget to inform Marcus about this," she added.

"Yes, yes," Fariq waved her away. "Come daily and practice. That is all you need."

Practice sounded good.

Only good that Alworth wasn't here, she told herself. He probably wouldn't be thrilled to hear about it at all.

CHAPTER 16

*P*en returned to Fariq's club the next morning. To her surprise, he had an entire room cleared out, including the carpets, and stood barefoot and without a shirt in the middle of the room.

Pen eyed him with misgiving. "What on earth are you doing?"

"I am practising Kalaripayattu. The oldest martial art in the world. The art of defence and attack that the warriors of old used. So effective that the British are trying to banish it. In vain."

He performed a choreography of smooth, fluent movements that were almost like a dance.

Pen watched with an open mouth. "This is amazing. I did not know you could do this."

"My father was an instructor, and I have been learning this since I was a child."

Pen watched, awe-struck, how he performed the fluid, elegant movements that were graceful yet simultaneously full of power.

"You should try it yourself one day," Fariq said as he wiped his face. "My father also taught women, you know."

"What happened to your father?" Pen sat on the floor and hugged her knees.

Fariq walked over to a little side table, lifted a jar and poured himself a glass of water. "They killed him in the uprising in Kerala."

"They. You mean the British."

Fariq bent his head in assertion.

"And then?"

"Seeing as they were persecuting everyone who knows and teaches Kalaripayattu, I tried to forget everything I've been taught and lived in the streets until His Grace found me."

"You never told me this before."

He handed her a glass of water, and Pen drank in big gulps. "Well, now you know."

"Fariq." She handed him the empty glass. "You know what they say about Marcus. Is it true?"

Fariq retied the sash around his waist and took his time to answer. "Some of it is. And some of it isn't."

Pen blew out air in frustration.

"If I am going to be honest, I think there are some devils inside that ride him. I don't know why. He is a man who—" He searched for words. "—simply hasn't found his peace. He's being driven by something." He gave her a quick grin. "Who knows in what den of iniquity he is now."

Pen looked at him miserably. "He's forgotten all about me, hasn't he?"

Fariq's eyes shifted away from her. "Of course he hasn't. He's just been very busy, that's all. Besides, I have good news. I found him yesterday."

Pen shot up. "What? How? Why didn't you tell me so earlier? Where is he?"

"In one of the dens of iniquity I talked about." He pulled on a coat.

Pen felt a range of emotions coursing through her. Relief, disappointment. Anger.

"Did you tell him about me? What does he say?" She shook his arm.

"Naturally, I told him about you. That you've grown up to be a man who's about to play the biggest gambling match the club has ever seen."

"And?" Pen pressed.

Fariq shrugged. "He laughed."

Pen took a moment to digest it. "That's it? He laughed?"

"You know how he is. He takes pleasure in the absurd."

Pen's face darkened. "Anything else he said?"

"He is certain you'd make a passable-looking boy."

"That is all? Nothing about his plans for me? What is going to happen to me?"

Fariq shifted in his chair uncomfortably. "Shiva's bones, I don't understand his behaviour, either," he muttered. "The only explanation I have is that he hasn't been himself in quite a while. If you ask me, Pen, let him be."

"How can I let him be? He is my guardian."

"The best thing is to make sure you craft your own path through life as best as possible. Some men are determined to walk down their course of self-destruction, and the best thing to do is to stay out of their way and to make sure they don't drag you down with him."

A cold knot formed in her stomach. "Where is he? I will go at once and talk to him." Pen jumped up.

"You can't save him, Pen." A sadness shadowed his face. "I've tried."

Pen shook her head. "You don't understand. I don't want to save him." Well, maybe a little. "I just want... an explanation."

"Pen, listen to me. Where he is now, you can't follow him. He will drag you down with him. You know it, too."

Their eyes met, and she slumped in defeat.

"I did manage to wheedle him into admitting that this situation of yours can't continue and that he needed to do something about you. He has agreed to send someone to pick you up. After the match."

"Pick me up? Why can't I just go to his home?"

"What do you think they would say if suddenly the Duke of Rochford had a lady living with him? Unchaperoned? Even if she is his ward. Even I know it's not the thing."

"In the past, it didn't matter."

"In the past, you were considerably younger. I daresay he needs to procure some kind of companion for you. No easy matter when you have no one to ask," Fariq grumbled.

"I am to live with a complete stranger?" Her fingers tensed in her lap.

Fariq shrugged. "Not too long. Once you come into your inheritance, I daresay you can do whatever you want."

She stood slumped over with a worried expression. "What a mess this is."

"There's no need to worry. I'll take care of you. In the worst case, I'll just have to marry you myself. We might make a good pair." He gave her a lopsided grin.

"And help you run the gaming salon?" Pen's smile did not reach her eyes.

"Why not?" He paused. "You'd hate every minute."

"I think I would." Pen rubbed her eyebrow. "It's kind of you to offer, but you know we wouldn't suit at all."

Fariq grinned at her, relieved. "I know. But now, let's play cards." He pulled out a pack of cards. "You need to practise. Do you remember the rules of picquet?"

They played for a good two hours, sitting cross-legged on the floor.

"See, you have not lost your touch. I lost three games."
Fariq collected the cards on the floor.

"Yes, but you won the rest." Pen crossed her arms with a
scowl.

"And you said I was a poor loser." Fariq grinned.

AFTERWARDS, PEN RETURNED TO HER LODGINGS. SHE
refreshed herself and left for White's. She found herself in a
dangerously morose mood, pondering on her fate and life in
general.

The icy knot in her stomach clenched tighter. What
would happen to her? What would she do? Where would she
live?

"What a muddle this is," she muttered.

"If you will excuse me, sir," a voice intruded into her
thoughts. The porter stood in front of her.

"I am wearing my best coat today," Pen started
defensively.

"No, no, sir. I merely meant I need to pick up the Philodendron here and need to move your armchair aside. The
poor plant has all but died. I wonder what ails it?"

Pen stared at the plant, which sported shrivelled and
dried yellow leaves.

"How very odd," the porter mourned, "when I took such
pains to water it regularly." He bore off the plant with a
doleful face.

Pen the plant killer. She struggled to maintain a straight
face and wondered where she should pour her brandy now.

CHAPTER 17

*A*lworth, who'd returned from Wiltshire three days ago, sat in the breakfast room of his club, reading the newspaper, and eating a plate full of beefsteak, potatoes, and kidney beans. He washed everything down with ale. He wondered where Pen was. The porter reported she'd been at the club on Tuesday, but not since then. He hadn't seen the boy—girl—brat—in, he counted, over a fortnight. She hadn't been at her lodgings when he'd passed by earlier, and she hadn't come to the club or to his house, either.

What was she up to? An odd feeling that he might pinpoint as being worried overcame him. Nonsense. He wasn't worrying about Pen, was he? He had no business worrying about Pen. None of his business at all.

To prove his point, he opened the *Spectator* to read, but reread the same paragraph several times.

Where on earth could that brat be? Nothing had happened to her, had it?

Just as he perused the announcement section, a portly man stepped up to his table.

"Alworth. A minute of your time."

Alworth looked up. "Pennington." Not his favourite person. But one needed to be polite, nonetheless.

"I wanted to ask for your advice. I've heard that Kumari's been your pupil."

"Indeed." Alworth lifted an eyebrow.

"So you know the boy. What about gaming? How good are the chances, really, of Kumari winning the match against Blackstone?"

Alworth blinked. "Did you say match?"

He laughed as if Alworth had made a jest. "Naturally. Where have you been? All of London is talking about it. It's even been recorded in the betting books of Perpignol's, as well as here, at White's."

"Indeed," murmured Alworth with an impassive face. "It seems I have been out of it. Perpignol's? By George."

"How good, would you say, are his skills at cards? The stakes are damnably high. I can't afford to lose."

"Might I have a look at the book?"

He brought the betting book over. Alworth perused it. Indeed, there was Pen's name. A duel of cards. And nearly all the gentlemen of the club have set wagers against him. A few for him. Alworth almost groaned.

So this is what Pen had been up to. While he himself had been busy in Wiltshire, she'd gotten herself set up for a duel of cards.

By George. The girl was thorough.

"My dear fellow, Kumari has a young and agile mind. He has considerable experience at cards despite his youth. In my opinion, Kumari therefore has the best chances of winning."

Pennington blanched. "I hope to prove you wrong. I have a considerable sum to lose if the milksop wins."

"That is too bad, Pennington. One should never underestimate milksops. When did you say it takes place?"

Pennington looked at his pocket watch. "Tomorrow evening."

Alworth swore. "Now, if you will excuse me. I have some urgent business to conduct."

HE FOUND PEN'S LODGINGS EMPTY, AS THEY HAD BEEN THE last three days. The landlady, a fat lady with a greasy apron, smacked her lips when she assessed Alworth.

"I can leave a message for him if it's urgent," she said, no doubt expecting to be bountifully reimbursed for her troubles.

"No, thank you. I will deliver the message myself," Alworth replied coolly. He stepped out of the house to wait, just when Pen disembarked from a hackney.

"Ah. Well met, Pen."

She looked startled when she beheld him. A rosy flush covered her cheeks. "Alworth. I didn't know you'd already returned. What are you doing here?"

"Waiting. For you." He took her by the arm and led her past the curious eyes of the landlady.

In her room, Pen dropped onto her chair, and gestured tiredly for him to sit. "I have nothing to offer in terms of refreshments."

"No matter." He studied her. She looked more dishevelled than usual, with one end of her shirt hanging out of her trousers, and her temples were matted with sweat.

"Did your trip to Wiltshire go well?" she asked awkwardly.

Only two weeks had passed since they'd last seen each other, and now they were conversing like strangers.

"Tolerably well, thank you. I have been seeking you for the past few days, in vain. You must be tremendously busy."

"Yes." She evaded his eyes.

"One hears all sorts of things," he drawled. "Do you care to tell me what is going on?"

She hesitated. He could almost see how her mind worked. Should she tell him? Shouldn't she? Could she trust him? Or better not?

His patience snapped.

"By Jove, Pen. This is no small matter, what has come to my ears. A gambling match at Perpignol's? Really?"

He hadn't intended for his anger to burst forth as it did. He was not a little surprised at himself. He never got angry. Why would he let this passion carry him away now?

Her eyes flew to his face. "You've heard of it?"

"It's all they ever talk about! By Jupiter." Alworth threw up his arms. "The entire *ton* will attend." Now it was Alworth's turn to get up and pace the room. "Blackstone is a hard-core gamester. He plays hard and deep. How on earth do you imagine you will win this match?"

"I have been playing cards my entire life. Besides, I've been training with Fariq."

"Fariq! I believe you have mentioned the name before, but I cannot recall who the blazes he is."

She made a tired gesture. "He owns the Perpignol."

Alworth stood thunderstruck. "The owner of the Perpignol!"

"Yes, yes. I know what you are going to say. A place of sin and vice. It's not as bad as you say. Truly."

"You've befriended the owner of the Perpignol. You actually went there. Alone." Alworth realised he sounded like a pedant.

"What if I did? It's none of your business. And, my lord, if you are quite done berating me, I would appreciate it if you stopped quizzing me on my motives. You are neither my father, nor my guardian, and I am not your ward."

Alworth exploded. "Thank the heavens for that! I am

starting to understand more and more why your guardian refuses to step into his role."

"And you, my lord, are a controlling, moralising prig."

Alworth took a big breath. He struggled with himself, shook his head, grabbed his hat and left the room without a word.

CHAPTER 18

The night of the gaming duel arrived. Pen's stomach had been queasy the entire day. She told herself this wasn't entirely the same as a real duel. A real duel was a matter of life and death; it involved pistols. This here was just a card game. Truth was, she'd had no idea at all what she'd let herself in for.

The eye of the entire gaming world was on her. Perpignol's had never been so full. When she entered, a murmur rose, and the men stepped aside, forming a small corridor to allow her to pass. Pen felt sweat pool in her armpits.

Fariq had arranged the gaming salon in such a manner that there was but a single table with two opposing chairs. A pack of picquet cards lay in its middle.

Taking a big breath, Pen pulled out the chair and sat. When another rumble of murmur arose, she knew Blackstone had arrived.

With a huff, he dropped into his chair. "Ready for the plucking?" he leered.

Pen's face remained deadpan. Rule number one in

gaming: never show your emotions. Pen cut the higher card, so she shuffled the pack and dealt.

Picquet required strategy, skill and an excellent memory, both for determining one's own discards, and for summing up the opponent's hand. Pen had a quick mind and the ability to accurately deduce her opponent's hand.

Blackstone, however, was no novice. He tended to take risks, and at first, it seemed luck was on his side.

"Carte blanche," he grinned during the exchange phase. This won him additional bonus points.

She lost heavily in the first round. There were five more deals to go. The air of excitement in the salon sizzled as they played the next deal.

Concentrate, Pen. Concentrate. She closed her eyes, took a big breath and attempted to cut out everyone in the room. Like Marcus had taught her. Tunnel vision. Only herself, her opponent and the game. Nothing else mattered.

Pen's advantage was that she was not the beginner Blackstone believed her to be. He became overconfident, and his discards were weak.

Seeing the smug smile on his face, she decided it was time to turn the tables. It was the last deal.

A tense, silent hush fell over the salon.

Pen's mind worked quickly. She dealt out her diamonds.

He discarded spades and hearts. Then he threw down a king.

Pen slouched back in her chair with a deep breath.

"Well?" He looked into the round with a triumphant, self-satisfied smirk.

"Well done, Blackstone," Pen breathed. A muttering rose in the room.

"I should've known the whelp was no good," a voice muttered, some concurred.

Pen raised a hand. The muttering subsided. "Well done," she repeated. "But, alas, not enough."

She threw down an ace.

Blackstone stared at it. Pen's totals ended up higher than his. A general roar erupted in the salon. People clapped her on the shoulder.

Fariq whooped.

She had won.

Her eyes roved over the crowd. There was no dark, curly head. Of course, Marcus would not come. But in the general hubbub, she imagined she'd seen a flash of pink in the corner of her eye. She turned her head.

Alworth.

His face was impassive. He didn't cheer her on, nor did he seem excited to be here. She felt a flush creep up her neck— then he was gone. Had she imagined it?

"I knew it! The boy would win! I always said so!"

Like in a dream, they stormed toward her and patted her on the back, the shoulders, tried to lift her up—

Until Fariq intervened. "Step back. Give him space, gentlemen. Give him space."

Pen sought out Alworth in the crowd, but she couldn't see him.

Instead, Fariq pushed her into his private study and closed the door.

"That went well," Fariq said, satisfied, as he walked across the room and opened a tapestry door in the wall. "Just as I said. You are brilliant! You're growing to be quite a celebrity. My offer stands. If you want to go into business with me, that is."

She gave him a tired smile. "Who knows? In the end, I may do just that. It's the only thing I seem to be good at. But now, all I want is to go home."

"You can get out the back door, where a coach is waiting for you." Fariq opened a side door.

She followed him through the dim hallway.

"He never came," she stated.

Fariq threw her a sympathetic look. "No."

"You know what, Fariq?" Pen said before she boarded the carriage. "I am thinking I really don't care anymore."

"I am sorry, Miss Pen," Fariq said. "I wish things were different."

As she reclined in the seat, she pondered on her words and felt that they were spoken true.

CHAPTER 19

*P*en felt she owed Alworth an apology. The knowledge that she'd incurred his wrath weighed heavily upon her. Had she jeopardised their friendship for good?

She went to Cavendish Square, and to her surprise, the butler said he was in.

"He is having supper and begs you to join him." He showed her the way to the dining room.

Alworth was eating beef stew and potatoes and merely raised an eyebrow when Pen entered.

She cleared her throat awkwardly. "May I join?" She felt like a school child asking for permission to sit.

He lifted a hand. "By all means."

Pen sat down at the edge of the chair and stole a look at him.

A heavy silence settled between them.

Alworth washed his beef down with a sip of the claret, then set down the cutlery. Finally, he said, "Congratulations on the win. London is talking of nothing else."

Pen cleared her throat. "I owe you an apology. I said some

dreadful things the other day. I didn't really mean them. I hope you are not offended."

"Offended? Me? My dear, it is, as you like to remind me, none of my business what you are up to. It's none of my business to know that you are a veritable prodigy in the gaming room. Have been trained to be one, possibly. Since your leading strings. Am I correct?" His grey eyes bore into hers like steel.

She swallowed hard, trying to manage a feeble answer. "Of sorts." Her shoulders sacked.

"Then I see no reason whatsoever why on earth you should feel beholden to tell me about every detail of your life, as well as your plans. Neither do I have to tell you about every detail about my life, and my plans, do I?"

"No. Of course not." Pen muttered. She stared at the intricate table decoration of fruits and flowers on the table without really seeing them.

He was different somehow. The usual amiable smile was on his face, but there was a distance between them, an aloofness that hadn't been there before. She stirred uneasily in her chair.

"Well. Then we are in agreement." Alworth's long, slim fingers drummed on the tablecloth.

Pen had a sudden urge to tell him everything. About her disguise. But then, he knew that already, didn't he? About Fariq, then. That it had all been his idea. How she'd been practicing her card skills. Sometimes until late into the night. About how she worried that this would be her life, because she was good for nothing else. But silence stretched, and the cold chasm between them grew.

"Well then, Pen. You had best retire and get some rest."

He was dismissing her.

Pen swallowed the clump in her throat. "Will I see you on the morrow?" She licked her dry lips. "We could go for a ride in Hyde Park. Or Vauxhall again. Or—maybe we could buy some more boots…." Her mind was a hot mess of confusion, and she needed the calm, soothing analysis of a friend.

"I am afraid I have a previous appointment. I am to take Miss Mountroy out for a ride." He pushed back his chair.

Pen ignored the quick stab of jealousy. "Miss Mountroy. How is the courtship going?"

"It is going well." His face was unreadable.

Pen stumbled up. "Well then. I'd better be going. I suppose I will see you at some point."

Walking swiftly along the streets, Pen felt she had to cool her mind and sort her thoughts, for she felt something had shifted in her relationship with Alworth.

But what? And why?

She hadn't even told him that Fariq had found Marcus.

Why did she still feel the stab in her heart when she thought of him riding out with Miss Mountroy?

Confound her and her blonde baby curls.

ALWORTH DROVE MISS MOUNTROY IN A CURRICLE THROUGH Hyde Park. His anger toward Pen hadn't ebbed. Maybe he was being unjust towards her. But he could not shake the feeling of hurt pride that she had not even bothered to tell him about the match, a match that all of London seemed to have been informed about. He should've paid more attention. He'd had more important matters to concern himself with than the gaming and betting in the clubs.

If he were honest with himself, he'd have to admit that maybe, just maybe, the gambling match wasn't really the issue at hand. The issue was deeper.

The issue of Pen not trusting in him.

Not confiding in him.

Not asking for his advice.

Why the deuce did he care so much about it?

They were only friends, he told himself.

A voice deep down told him that wasn't entirely true.

He shifted uneasily as Miss Mountroy lisped on. By George, what was she saying now? How purple velvet curtains were better than gauze ones. Was she already trying to redecorate his home?

"Wouldn't you agree, my lord?" She fixed her violet eyes on him. The eyes of a porcelain doll. Pretty, but rather vapid.

Exactly like he wanted his wife to be. Yet he couldn't shake the vision of another set of eyes. Huge, dark brown pools fringed with long black eyelashes. Mysterious and soulful, they turned fiery when angered, sparkled when she smiled, but in its depth, there was sadness...

"Er. Yes." He heard himself say.

She clapped her hands. "Splendid," she lisped.

He had no idea what he'd just agreed to.

"Mama will be so pleased when she hears you are to attend the Whittlesborough Ball. Do you think," she clasped her hands, "do you think they will let me dance–the waltz?" She looked at him expectantly.

Dash it, the Whittlesborough Ball. He may have received an invitation. The chit no doubt expected him to reserve a dance with her. Which was what he must have agreed to just now.

She beamed at him the entire way home.

Alworth noted that her constant smiling made him feel grumpy.

He found Pen's distempered berating of his person to be more refreshing.

Decidedly out of sorts, he concluded he needed to get rid of Miss Letty Mountroy and shift his attention to more pressing matters. Boots. Yes. He could go buy some more boots.

CHAPTER 20

*P*en arrived at her lodgings dejected. Her discussion with Alworth hadn't gone as she intended, but if she asked herself what she'd expected, she couldn't say, either.

Maybe Alworth was right, and she needed a nap.

The landlady at the Dancing Willow looked up from polishing the glasses when she stepped in. "I let her in," she said.

"Who?"

"The lady."

"What lady?" Could she mean one of her friends? Lucy or Arabella? Pen took two steps at a time up the stairs. Her heart hammered in anticipation.

She tore the door open.

She stumbled over her trunk, which stood, packed, by the door.

"What—Who?"

Pen's eyes flew to the woman who sat in a chair by the window. She got up. A pretty, dainty lady with chestnut brown hair wearing a dark green pelisse. She was a stranger. Disappointment hit her that she wasn't one of her friends.

"Who are you?" Pen took a step towards her. "And what are you doing in my room?"

"I apologise, Miss Reid. I know it must appear to you to be a gross invasion of your privacy. But the landlady could not tell me when you would return, and she was kind enough to let me wait here." She lifted a hand. "My name is Mrs Charlotte Wentwood."

Pen eyed her with mistrust. "I don't know any Charlotte Wentwood. Why are you here? Did Miss Hilversham send you?" Then it hit her that she'd called her Miss Reid.

"No. Although you are correct that I have been sent by a very good friend we both share. I was asked to offer you hospitality and guidance. I would be your companion and help guide your way back into society."

Pen felt exhaustion flood through her. "Who exactly sent you? Lucy? I mean, the Duchess of Ashmore?"

Mrs Wentwood hesitated. "The friend requests to remain anonymous. I may reveal he is a male, and he has only the best of intentions towards you. He wishes you to accept with goodwill his sponsorship; however, he insists his identity must, for reasons of propriety, remain hidden."

Pen's eyes flew up to meet hers. "Marcus." It had to be. Fariq had said he'd send someone.

Mrs Wentwood bit on her lips and looked away.

That reaction confirmed Pen's suspicion. Marcus wasn't quite the wicked person she'd thought he was. He was making sure she was taken care of. He cared about her reputation. Wanted to help her find her way back into society. Obviously, that couldn't happen if she was taken under the wing of the Wicked Duke. So, he'd sent her a lady companion. A chaperone.

Relief flushed through her, not because she cared about

joining society, but because Marcus had finally done something for her.

"Tell me, does he not want his identity known because of his–his–reputation? Because he is afraid it will rub off on me?"

Mrs Wentwood hesitated. "I am not to talk about your sponsor at all. Know that he is a person of considerable wealth and influence, so certainly, reputation plays a role."

"What does he want me to do?"

"You are to have a season."

Pen dropped onto her bed. "A season? But why?"

Mrs Wentwood smiled. "Because that is what young ladies of your age are expected to have. They have a season, so they can find a suitable match to marry."

Pen crossed her arms. "I don't want to marry."

"I have been told your reaction would be thus." Mrs Wentwood got up and shook out her skirts.

"A season. You mean with balls and the like?" Precisely what Pen did not want.

"Balls, routs, parties, picnics. Your sponsor insists that only the best will do. No expenses are to be spared."

Pen scratched her head. "I don't know. I'm not terribly good in social situations."

"Please don't do that," Mrs Wentwood said gently. "Scratching your head. And no one is good in social situations unless they practise their social skills."

"What if I decline?"

"You won't."

Pen looked at her, confused. "And why won't I decline?"

"Because, as I understand it, your biggest desire currently is a reunion with your guardian, am I correct?"

Their eyes met. Pen nodded.

"Then you must understand that this reunion depends on you entering the season—as a lady."

She as good as gave away that Marcus was the sponsor. A mix of contradictory emotions coursed through Pen. Relief that her charade was finally over. Resistance to be turned into a simpering lady. A sparkle of excitement at the thought of dancing at a ball. And resignation.

"You must forgive me, but I have taken the liberty to pack your belongings. I do not believe you will need many of them. But as they are yours, it is understood they will be taken along." Mrs Wentwood attempted to lift the trunk.

Pen jumped up, and like a true gentleman, took the trunk from her.

"I see it will be a considerable amount of work," Mrs Wentwood said pensively.

"What is?"

"To turn you back into a girl."

Mrs Charlotte Wentwood's husband was very busy and rarely at home, she told Pen in the carriage on the way to her home.

"I daresay George barely knows what his father looks like," Mrs Wentwood added.

"George?"

"My little son. He is three. And a rascal." A smile lit up her face, and she looked beautiful.

"Mrs Wentwood. I just want you to know that I appreciate what you are doing for me. But it will be quite in vain. I have no social manners at all, and I am determined not to marry. I am only doing this because I want to be reunited with my guardian."

"Please call me Charlotte." She smiled, and a dimple appeared in her cheek. "And I may call you Penelope, yes? I agree you will be quite a challenge, but I like challenges. I have given my promise to help you and help you I will."

"But why? You don't even know me."

"No, I don't. But I know the friend we both share. I am doing this for my friend."

There it was again. Friend. Pen wondered what kind of relationship, exactly, Marcus and Charlotte had that she would go out of her way to help a complete stranger. He must've offered her a considerable amount of money for such a favour, she concluded. On the other hand, she herself would also do anything for her friends if they asked her. Without blinking.

"Is this really what he wants? That I am a girl again?"

"Oh yes. More than anything. He requires your dedicated participation."

"If, say, I am successful in having a season, will your—our —friend then agree to come out of his incognito? So I may meet and talk to him?"

Charlotte weighed her head back and forth. "We haven't talked about it. But I suppose why not."

Pen's face brightened.

"The stories I have heard about you! Is it true you took part in a duel?"

Pen told her about the incident with Blackstone and then the card match later.

Charlotte shuddered. "I cannot possibly imagine how you held yourself up in these situations. I don't know whether to admire your courage. Or is it foolishness? It is good you are leaving all this behind."

The carriage slowed and stopped in front of an elegant townhouse in Berkeley Square. "Ah, here we are."

Pen felt ill at ease entering a stranger's house.

She was shown a beautiful room on the upper floor, femininely decorated in cream and pale pink. She'd never seen such a pretty room. Mrs Wentwood—Charlotte—had impeccable taste. She also had a will of iron.

"Now. The first thing we must do is go to the dressmaker. However, not in this outfit. You will have to take it off." She threw Pen a look that would've left Wellington's army quaking.

"What. Now?" Pen was flustered.

"Yes. Now." Charlotte gave a sign to a maid and crossed her arms. "I am waiting."

Pen undressed with the maid's help, feeling self-conscious and awkward. Charlotte clucked. "Take it all away and have it washed and donated. You won't be needing them anymore."

"No! Not donated. Please. They're not my clothes. I need to return them." This was only half true, for surely Sally's brother did not expect to have his clothes returned, but she felt she could not get rid of her male attire just yet. "Please."

"But we will have an entire wardrobe made for you so you will not need it anymore."

"Nonetheless, they're mine, and I want to keep them." Pen's will was as strong as Charlotte's. "If you intend to give my clothes away, this stops right here, and I will not take part in anything else you have in mind for me."

She relented. "Very well. What a hard head you have. Speaking of heads, we will have to do something about your hair." She touched Pen's badly cropped mane and frowned. "We will have to get you some hair pieces on the side and on the back."

"A wig?" Pen would hate wearing a wig.

"Not entirely. It might be sufficient if we attach some curls on either side, and a little in the back." She pursed her lips. "It would have to be in the exact same black hair colour. Let's see what Ellie says. She is my abigail and excellent with hair."

Charlotte lent her an apple green afternoon dress which was embroidered at the hem, a pair of matching shoes, and a shawl. Ellie fiddled around with her hair and stuck a countless number of pins into her head. It felt heavy.

When she looked into the mirror, she gaped at herself. Curls framed her face and an elegant, but fake chignon crowned her head. It made her neck look swanlike.

This was not Pen, the gangly youth, but Penelope. A lady.

Charlotte clapped. "What did I say? Ellie, you can truly work miracles. Oh, but look at you! You are beautiful. The hairpieces are slightly lighter than your hair, it is so very black. It will do for now, and we will try to find more appropriate pieces on our shopping trip later."

Ellie had indeed wrought a miracle with her cropped mane. She looked like she wore her hair up in the current fashion, with curls framing her narrow face, emphasising her high cheekbones and luscious eyes.

"I look—look—like one of those brainless fainting damsels," Pen complained.

Before she'd cropped her locks, she had worn her heavy, long hair pulled straight back in a bun. It had been a plain and sensible hairstyle that had suited her at the seminary. Now she looked silly and frivolous, like she couldn't put two sentences together. Maybe she should start lisping like Miss Mountroy, Pen thought disgustedly.

"You look absolutely gorgeous. Like a young lady should. Like the princess you are."

Charlotte knew about Pen's family history. She said she felt honoured to help Pen transform back into a princess. Pen, however, shrugged it off. Princess, bah. It was another one of those things about her identity that seemed vague, like being British, or Indian, or both, or neither. Ultimately, she did not know what it meant, or whether it should even mean anything in terms of who she really was. Why couldn't she just be plain Pen?

Alworth had understood that, hadn't he?

She sighed.

"Chin up. Smile! Oh, the colour of your dress brings out touches of green in your dark brown eyes. How well it suits you!" Charlotte tugged at the shawl, pleased.

"My hair normally never curls like that."

"Probably not, but no matter, these fake curls are excellent. After your hair has grown back, we will tackle the problem again, but for now this will do very well."

Charlotte grasped her hands and drew her out of her chair. "Off we go. We have much to accomplish on Bond Street."

CHAPTER 21

*W*ho knew a properly outfitted lady needed so many things?

Petticoats, reticules, shawls, shoes, stockings, bonnets, gloves, morning dresses, afternoon dresses, dresses for riding, carriage dresses, pelisses, spencers, ball gowns (three), umbrellas, nightgowns and more.

Pen's head whirled.

She'd let Charlotte and the dressmaker decide on fabric and colour. She'd only put down her foot once when she refused to have her ballroom gown made in cotton candy pink with pink roses and insisted on a simple cream dress. Charlotte tilted her head to the side and agreed that the simple cream would suit Pen's complexion admirably.

Pen couldn't get Alworth out of her mind. What would he think now that Pen had completely disappeared? Had he left a message? Ought she to leave him a message? Did it even matter? Maybe he was quite relieved to finally be rid of her. Yet, she had not said goodbye to him. She felt a pang. What to do?

She'd tried to convince Charlotte to stop at the Dancing

Willow to ask whether messages had been left for her. But Charlotte would have none of it.

"Out of the question. The last time you were there, they knew you as a man. You cannot return as a woman. Even though they would, likely, not recognise you."

"But what if I have missives waiting there for me?" Pen thought, in particular, of messages from Alworth.

"We can send a footman to collect them." Charlotte straightened Pen's fichu, which had slipped out of her décolleté. Pen detested that garment because it itched, and it always wound up crooked.

Pen grumbled but agreed Charlotte had a point and sending a footman was the more sensible notion.

Her heart thudded against her ribcage when the footman, indeed, returned with a missive, which he handed to her on a silver platter. It was from Alworth.

She broke the seal and opened it with shaking hands.

Pen.
> Where the deuce are you?
> I await you at the club tonight at eight.
> A.

She folded the missive again, thoughtfully.

"We do not have any plans tonight, do we?" Pen asked Charlotte.

"Oh yes. Tonight, we are to dine at the Hadlows. It will be an excellent opportunity for you to practise your social skills. And tomorrow, we have breakfast at Lady Sheringham's. The day after, there is a ball at the Whittlesboroughs, which we must attend, of course. It is a very important event. Say, Penelope. Are you listening?"

"Hm? Yes. Of course. Breakfast at Whittlesboroughs and a ball at Lady Sheringham's."

"Wrong. The other way around. You seem rather preoccupied with something?"

Pen could hardly tell her she was trying to figure out how to sneak out of the house in her boy's clothes so she could meet Alworth at White's at eight.

"At what time is this dinner tonight?"

"At eight."

Her heart sank. "And how long will it last?"

"Who knows?" Charlotte said brightly. "If they decide to have a musical interlude, which is likely, or even some dancing, it could be until midnight."

Pen's shoulders sagged. It looked unlikely that she'd be able to meet Alworth tonight.

DINNER AT THE HADLOWS WAS A TERRIFYING AFFAIR. SHE knew absolutely no one. A room full of strange faces looked at her with polite curiosity. Charlotte took her by the arm and introduced her to everyone, and Pen had a hard time remembering all the names and faces. She was unconscious that she drew attention with her dark beauty that contrasted to the simplicity of her evening gown. She looked lithe and elegant, and her absent-mindedness came across as aloofness. Many a male guests compared her to an orchid.

"Reid, you said her name is?" Lady Billingstone fixed her lorgnette at Pen.

"A certain Captain Reid was once stationed in Rajasthan." Viscountess Rawleigh replied. She bent her head toward Lady Billingstone as she whispered, "They say he eloped with an Indian princess and turned Indian himself. I remember reading the tale in the *Morning Chronicles*. It was the story of the day. So romantic!"

"She has clearly inherited her mother's complexion," Lady Billingstone noted.

"Yet, she is not entirely Indian, is she?" Two lorgnettes fixed on her as if she were the most interesting specimen in the room, which she no doubt was.

Pen rolled her eyes and wished she were back in her trousers. She'd felt gauche in trousers, too, but at least they'd been comfortable to wear. Her corset was too tight, and her satin slippers pinched.

She was dreadfully bored in this company. Yet, to please Charlotte, she smiled, was polite, picked at her food and nodded at the right places when her table partner, Vicar Padlow, tried to converse with her about the merits of crop rotation.

Pen wondered whether that was to be her fate from now on. Boring supper parties until she received a marriage proposal. Was that what Marcus intended? To marry her off? It would certainly solve his problems. He'd be rid of a ward who'd been nothing but a nuisance to him, and she'd be married to someone like Vicar Padlow, who had clammy hands, greasy lips and a nasal voice.

After Lady Hadlow led the ladies out of the supper room to the parlour for tea, the general conversation changed.

"Did you hear the latest news about Viscount Alworth?" a woman with a purple turban spoke up.

Pen nearly dropped her cup of tea in her lap.

"I heard he is to marry Miss Mountroy. Miss Letty Mountroy."

Her daughter, Miss Patricia, a plump girl in an unflattering pink silk dress, sighed.

"How vexatious. Another eligible bachelor to scratch off the list. The Indian prince, too, has disappeared."

Pen, who'd just taken a sip from her tea, coughed.

"Do you happen to know him, Miss Reid? He seems to be a fellow countryman of yours."

"Erm, no. I haven't had the pleasure." She mumbled from behind her napkin.

"What a shame. There aren't too many eligible gentlemen left now."

To Pen's relief, the general topic of conversation then switched to fashions and silks, and the newest fashion plates in *La Belle Assemblée.*

After supper, Pen stepped up to Charlotte, who was conversing with Lady Hadlow.

"Here you are, child." She took Pen's hands between hers and patted them. "You look somewhat white around the nose. Are you feeling the thing?"

"I have a dreadful headache," Pen replied, rubbing her temple. It felt like a blacksmith hammered against the anvil that was her brain.

Charlotte regarded her. "Maybe this has been too much for you," she said to Pen's surprise. "Let us retire early, then. You need to be well-rested for tomorrow. I will give our excuses to Lady Hadlow."

Pen could've hugged her.

Back in Berkeley Square, she drank some valerian tea, crawled into her bed and waited for the maid to leave. She counted to a hundred, then crawled out again, dug out her boy's clothes from the bottom drawer, dressed in a hurry, and opened the window, which faced the back courtyard. Pen peered down. Climbing out of windows was becoming a routine. She could do this.

Pen held onto the parapet gutter and sidled down the pipe. She swung herself with ease over the fence and strode down the road.

. . .

WHITE'S WAS FULL AT THAT TIME OF THE NIGHT. THE EVENING had degenerated into drinking and gambling. But Pen could not find Alworth in any of the rooms.

"He's not here, sir," the porter said when she asked him. "But he left a message for you." He handed Pen a missive.

> Pen:
>
> *I am deeply disappointed. I will make one last attempt to meet you, and, if that should fail, I depart for India without saying farewell.*
>
> *The Whittlesborough ball tomorrow.*
>
> A.

Pen crumpled the paper and groaned.

How on earth was she to accomplish that? Of course she would attend the Whittlesborough ball tomorrow.

As a lady.

CHAPTER 22

*T*he Right Honourable the Viscount Alworth.

My Lord,

    Pray forgive me. I never meant any of this. If you only knew—

Alworth,

    I do miss your friendship! Your company and anecdotes, your smile—

Dear Alworth,

    This is terrible. I am a girl now, and Charlotte Wentwood is dragging me to every single social event! I don't have a single minute to myself. The women gossip, and the men ogle me like a piece of flesh for sale on the market. They are all pig-widgeons. I keep looking for you, but you are never there. Marcus isn't, either. You're right, he's not worthy of a guardian, a friend – and I hate him! I've taken your friendship for granted, and I am so, so sorry! I wish we could meet so I could tell you—

Dear Archie,

Please, please, please don't marry that terrible Miss Letty Mountroy.

She has translucent eyes like a fish, and she lisps.

PEN CRUMPLED UP THE PAPER AND THREW THE FOURTEENTH ball of paper into the fireplace and watched it burn to a crisp.

The Whittlesborough ball was tonight, and she was a nervous wreck.

Somehow, she had to accomplish the impossible.

She had to attend as both Pen and Penelope!

How on earth was she to accomplish that?

She'd heavily bribed a footman to take her bag with her men's clothes and hide it under a bush in the Whittlesborough's garden. Somehow, she'd have to sneak out, find the bag, and transform herself to Pen, meet Alworth and explain.

As easy as pie.

Pen snorted. The hardest part may well be having to explain to Alworth.

Explain what?

She did not know what to explain, or how, but she felt down to the marrow of her bones that if she did not meet and talk to Alworth at the ball, she would lose his friendship forever.

She'd considered meeting him as Penelope. It would be the easiest solution. He would see her in her ballgown anyhow. But confront him in petticoats? The thought made her lose all courage. She had more self-confidence when she was the boy Pen. She'd known Alworth when wearing trousers. Ergo, it seemed fitting that she would have this last conversation with him in her disguise.

Something heavy lodged in her breast at the thought, and she could not identify what it was. It had been sitting there ever since they'd last talked, when she'd missed the opportunity to come clean with him. Ever since Alworth had looked at her in that odd way, as though he'd expected her to trust him, and she didn't. It wasn't disappointment, precisely. But a slight sadness. Like he hadn't expected anything else from her to begin with.

The look had nearly killed her.

Pen chewed at the tip of her quill.

Trust. It was a two-edged sword. When you trust someone, it makes you vulnerable. She knew, deep down, that she could trust Alworth. So, why didn't she?

Because she was afraid he'd treat her differently.

If she were a woman again, would he treat her like that terrible Miss Letty Mountroy? Look down on her with that patronising smile, not take her seriously? She would hate it if he ever treated her like that.

She'd seen them from a distance in Hyde Park in the morning.

"Oh look, there's Alworth with his fiancée," Charlotte had said, and pointed to a dashing sporting curricle that drove speedily along the avenue.

Miss Mountroy, with her purple bonnet, was chattering, and Alworth had his face turned towards her and smiled that charming smile of his.

Pen had felt a fierce stab in her heart that took her breath away.

It wasn't mere jealousy. It was a poisoned barb right in her heart that, if she pulled it out, would leave a definite hole.

Pen had yanked her bonnet down over her face and turned aside when they passed. Her heart hammered, her palms were sweaty, and she wondered whether this overall feverish feeling that had taken hold of her body meant that she was falling ill.

This was Alworth, she told herself. So there should be no reason at all why her heart was leaping out of her chest, knowing he was nearby. He was just Alworth, and granted, she hadn't seen him for several weeks, and she missed him. She missed his friendship, his easy laughter, the sleepy smile in his eyes, the sarcastic tilt around his lips. She missed his wit, and dash it, even his pink waistcoat.

She missed him—well—almost in the same way she used to miss Marcus, with every fibre of her being.

Pen stood stock still.

Charlotte pulled on her arm and continued chattering, not noticing that Pen's world had just tilted.

Pen wondered whether he'd have recognised her in her pale-yellow walking dress and corkscrew curls. So far, none of the club acquaintances had as much as blinked in recognition when she'd met them at various soirees and breakfasts. Granted, there hadn't been too many, and only one had enquired whether she might, possibly, be the sister to That Indian Prince Who'd Brought Blackstone to his Knees (and what an excellent game that had been!) and who'd vanished a month ago.

The maid entered to prepare her bath.

Pen set down her quill.

There was no purpose to writing a missive. She had to go to the ball to meet him and talk to him herself.

CHAPTER 23

The Whittlesborough event was the season's ball of balls. Lady Whittlesborough liked to boast every year that the ball was an even bigger squeeze than the year before. One could hardly dance, and this year, she vowed, it shall be even more so.

Pen was wearing a gorgeous confection of gauze and pale silk with golden embroidery.

"You look like a goddess," Charlotte had breathed. "If you don't get a proposal tonight, then I don't know what is wrong with the gentlemen."

She herself looked beautiful in a night blue gown that showed off her creamy décolleté, her fair hair elegantly coiffed to a chignon, with curls teased out.

Her husband, a tall, broad man, attended as well. Pen found she had a lot in common with him. Neither seemed to enjoy small talk.

"Will is a bit shy," Charlotte had explained with a laugh. "I expect him to spend most of the night in the card room, but you owe both Pen and me at least one dance. Do you hear, Will?"

"Of course, my dear." He looked down at his wife affectionately, and she returned his smile.

Pen watched them wistfully. Aside from her parents, she had never seen two people so much in love. It was there, in every glance, in every movement. In the gentleness with which he placed the shawl around Charlotte's shoulders. In the way his eyes softened when he looked at her.

How lucky Charlotte was.

THE WHITTLESBOROUGH MANSION WAS ABLAZE WITH LIFE AND light. The path leading up to it was lit with torches. Flower garlands interwoven with ivy decorated the staircase leading up to the ballroom. The strains of violins rang from the ballroom. A quadrille started.

Pen clenched the fan in her gloved hands and moistened her dry lips.

"Nervous?" Charlotte stepped up to her.

Pen nodded.

"There is no need. But I recall how nervous I was at my first ball. I met Will there. How long ago that was! Granted, your introduction to society is unconventional." Charlotte reached out to straighten Pen's dress and readjusted the flower braided into her hair. "Traditionally, you should've been presented at court first, together with the other debutantes. But no matter. Everything about you is unconventional, but never let it be said that you're not a diamond of the first water. Because you are." Charlotte's warm eyes were on her.

Pen felt a clump in her throat. She felt she did not deserve this praise. "Thank you," she whispered. "I know I am difficult sometimes, but I want you to know that I do appreciate everything you do for me."

"Oh, Pen. You're making me tear up," Charlotte said with

a tremulous smile. "Well then, let us proceed to the ballroom."

Charlotte took her husband's arm, Pen his other, and the three of them stepped up to Lord and Lady Whittlesborough, who stood by the entrance to the ballroom to greet them.

Pen searched the room. This time, she was not looking for a curly black head, but a well-coiffed blond one. A tall, athletic figure with proud bearing. Her heart quickened, then stopped.

He was dancing with a girl in pale blue. Miss Letty Mountroy. Alworth himself was finely dressed, his coat and breeches moulded to his athletic body. He wore a silver embroidered waistcoat and a single red flower in the button-hole. The cuffs gleamed white against his dark coat. He was exquisite. She wouldn't have expected anything less. And he danced gracefully. They made a beautiful couple. Miss Mountroy's mother seemed to think so, too, for she watched from the side with a group of other matrons, beaming proudly.

Pen struggled to breathe evenly. Her corset squeezed her lungs.

Charlotte introduced her to a gentleman, who asked her for the next dance. Pen nodded and took his hand automatically. She had not even registered his name. Her partner led her onto the dance floor, and everything went by in a dizzying, colourful whirl.

ALWORTH RECOGNISED HER THE MINUTE SHE ENTERED THE ballroom. He almost stepped on Miss Mountroy's feet and missed the next step.

By Jove. Could it be possible that the awkward, angular boy turned out to be such a graceful lady? Dressed in cream and silk, she stepped lithely into the room, on the arm of

Colonel Wentwood. She bore herself proudly. Her dark head was elegantly coiffed, with a golden band skilfully woven through a braid that crowned the top of her head with flowers. Her neck was long, her dark eyes large. She was like a slender, delicate lily. Every inch a princess.

"Beautiful," he murmured.

Miss Mountroy batted her eyelashes at him, giggled and blushed.

Alworth flashed a smile at her, suppressing an oath. Would this cursed dance never end?

He saw Pen did not lack in dancing partners, either.

He bowed to Miss Mountroy and returned her to her mother, Lady Mountroy, who looked upon him with a maternal, possessive look that was confident of her daughter's matrimonial victory.

Alworth felt his coat was too tight.

He bowed to the ladies, turned and strolled away.

Right into the arms of Serena, who stood by the window, smiling at him.

"Well met, Serena." He murmured. "Your husband?"

"In the card room, as usual."

Serena was a vision in indigo blue. Her eyes sparkled. Yes, Alworth mused, he had been right to worship the ground she walked on. Once upon a time.

"He is neglecting you most shamefully." Alworth bowed. "He has no reason to complain, then, when I whisk his beautiful wife away for a dance."

She touched his arm playfully with her fan. "You are an incorrigible flirt. And a rogue. I see you have been dancing with the Mountroy girl."

"Hm. Yes." He led her to the dance floor.

"Rumours say that you are to be engaged." She lifted an elegantly plucked eyebrow. "However, I have found that rumours, especially regarding you, tend to be unreliable. So tell me."

"My dear. I have only danced a dance with her. Once. It may have been twice. I forget. And now society expects the banns to be called. What can I say? I shall be dragged to the altar by those zealous Mamas. Behold me, struggling in vain."

"Archie." She frowned. "Be serious."

He twirled her around.

"But I am always serious. Especially with you."

"You are not. I know you too well. You always joke when the topic becomes serious."

The corners of his mouth tilted up. "You have always known me too well, Serena."

"Yes. But like a very good childhood friend, or like a naughty little brother whom I need to keep an eye on all the time."

"So you keep reminding me." He made an exaggerated wince and placed a hand over his heart.

Serena rolled her eyes. "We both know you are well beyond that."

"Do we?" He smiled at her wistfully.

"Archie. You have never really forgiven me, have you? For marrying William."

His mocking eyes turned serious. "I am mortally jealous of him. Of you two together. You are the perfect pair. You know I would never begrudge you any happiness, Serena. You belong with him."

She cast a brilliant smile on him.

"And Pen?" She twirled about him again. "What about her?"

"What about Pen?" He lifted his head to look for Pen. She was dancing at the other end of the line with a gentleman. "She is doing well? I see she lacks no partner."

"She is doing well?" Serena mimicked his tone. "Is that all

you have to say? She is brilliant. Her transformation is miraculous. The gentlemen are falling all over themselves to lead her to the dance floor."

"If you say so, you must, no doubt, be correct." A sarcastic little smile played about his mouth. "She will litter the ballroom floor with broken hearts, then."

She hit him again with her fan. "Do be serious, Archie."

He sobered. "You did an excellent job, Serena. Thank you."

Serena's eyes were troubled. "I have to admit, I did it at first only to do you a favour. And, I was, of course, dying with curiosity. You never ask anyone for favours, do you, Archie? So, when you came to my home to solicit my help for a friend of yours, and told me her fascinating and touching story, and asked me to be her chaperone, I was more than willing to do it. But, Archie, in the meantime, I have grown fond of the girl. Very fond. Therefore, I need to ask you, as a good friend, what your intentions are towards her. Because I would hate to see her hurt."

The glint of humour left his eyes. "My intentions? As you have repeatedly impressed upon me, you know me rather well, so it would come as no surprise to you that I am an egotistical creature. My intentions are simple. I intend to amuse myself. And it is infinitely amusing to see a girl who's masqueraded about as a boy the past two months be turned into a princess." He mused. "There is something charming about it."

"Balderdash." The music stopped, and she curtsied as he bowed. "I think you do not know your own heart to see the truth."

"You are so full of wisdom tonight, Serena. Pray, what is the truth?"

"The truth, my friend, is that you have fallen head over heels in love with her, of course." She tapped him with her fan on his sleeve. "Mind you. Not the infatuated puppy love you had for me. This might very well be the real thing."

With a knowing smile, Mrs Charlotte Serena Wentwood turned to find her husband.

The mocking reply died on his lips as he remained behind, frozen on the dance floor.

CHAPTER 24

*P*en was restless.

She'd seen from the corner of her eyes how Alworth and Charlotte had danced, but they'd been at the other end of the line, and her partner had talked continuously. It was difficult to concentrate both on the jabbering of her partner, and on the pair at the other end of the line.

At first, she could barely believe her eyes. Charlotte knew Alworth? They not only knew each other, they talked and laughed as if they were best friends. It even looked like they flirted. Charlotte touched him at the arm and looked deeply into his eyes. And did she just bat her eyelashes? And Alworth smiled down at her like she was the most beautiful woman in the room.

An ugly snake slithered in the pit of her stomach. Nonsense. He looked like that at all women.

Except for her, of course.

Somehow, she'd have to leave the ballroom, sneak out into the garden, find the bag, transform herself to Pen, find Alworth, stutter forth an apology, then transform herself back into a girl.

That this was bound to be a disaster was assured. She hoped Charlotte would forgive her.

At the end of the dance, her partner brought her a glass of chilled lemonade, which she drank gratefully. The strains of a quadrille started, and a red-haired gentleman, she'd forgotten his name, bowed in front of her, claiming his dance. Pen placed her hand on his arm to be led to the floor, yet immediately hedged a plan on how she could get rid of him so she could sneak out into the garden.

The music broke off suddenly, and a hush fell over the room.

"By Jove," her partner uttered.

What was going on? Why was everyone staring at the entrance? Her gaze flew to the door, and she gasped.

A tall man, with black unruly hair and green flashing eyes, surveyed the room. Beautiful, degenerate, and slightly drunk. Lucifer manifested.

The Duke of Rochford had arrived.

PEN STOOD AS IMMOBILE AS LOT'S WIFE AFTER SHE WAS transformed into a salt pillar.

Marcus. After years and years of yearning for him, when she expected to see him the least, there he suddenly stood.

He was so different from how she remembered him.

Her first impression was that he'd grown old. His temples were greyed, his face pasty and slightly bloated, his eyes bloodshot. He had a slight paunch but carried himself well in the dark evening attire.

"Don't mind me." He lifted a hand like a king, pulling his lips to a lop-sided smile. "Resume, my good people. Resume." He strolled languidly down the stairs towards the card room.

"I wonder why he is here," a lady behind her said shrilly.

"He must be on the prowl again. Ladies, keep a close eye on your daughters. No one is safe, I say. No one!"

Pen turned, astonished at the effect Marcus had on the people.

Her first instinct was to run after him into the card room. Instead, the music resumed with an increased volume of gossip and chatter, and she allowed herself to be led into the next dance. Her movements were stiff as her thoughts tumbled through her mind.

It was clear why he was here.

He was here for her, of course.

Her debutante ball.

He was her sponsor. He hadn't forgotten.

Hadn't Charlotte said she was to avoid her sponsor at any cost? Piffle. She needed to talk to him.

"I am rather tired, and my feet hurt," she said as she pulled her partner aside. "How about a game of cards, yes? Let's go to the card room. Let's play a round of picquet." She dragged her partner, who was completely taken by surprise, toward the card room.

"But, Miss Reid, I have promised the next dance to Miss Venish…." he stuttered.

Pen ignored him and let her eyes roam the card room for Marcus. She opened her fan and fanned herself. Why was it so deucedly hot all of a sudden? And where was he? A feeling of vexation flushed through her. Why was he forevermore a step ahead of her, and she always running after him?

In the very back of the room was movement. Just in the nick of time, Pen saw that a tapestry door was closing shut.

"There. We will go there." Pen pointed at the tapestry door.

Her partner flushed beet red. "But Miss Reid. We can't."

"Why ever not?"

He swallowed; his Adam's apple bobbed in his throat.

"It is entirely improper," he hissed, his eyes dashing to the right and left to make sure that no one saw them.

"Piffle," Pen said.

"Miss Reid. I must insist."

"You may go."

"Excuse me?"

Pen waved her hand. "You are dismissed. Go."

The man stuttered. "But Miss Reid…" He stumbled an apology and left.

He is an idiot, Pen thought as she turned to the tapestry door.

"Beauty in distress?" a familiar low voice murmured into her ear.

Pen whirled around.

Alworth.

He looked at her with sleepy, amused eyes. Her stomach somersaulted.

Then he bowed. "Miss Reid? Alworth is my name. Forgive my presumptuousness by not waiting for an official introduction."

She blinked at him. But didn't he know that she was Pen? So why was he pretending otherwise? What charade was this? Now she had to pretend they'd never met before.

She curtsied.

Looking up at him, she suddenly found him rather closer than expected.

She smelled his cologne. She could count every single fine hair on his eyelashes.

Something hot and sizzling rushed through her veins as their eyes met.

"Miss Reid." There was an odd, intense look on his face. "Would you like to dance?"

Alworth was asking her for a dance? Now? "No. I have

danced enough. I need to go in there." She pointed at the red tapestry door. "I want to explore what is in there."

Both his eyebrows shot up. "Are you quite certain?"

"Absolutely."

She pulled the knob and opened the door.

Let him come or let him stay. She would go inside.

Alworth followed. The door closed behind them.

Pen's first impression was that everything was scarlet.

The walls of the narrow hallway where they found themselves. The carpet on the floor. The air was heavy with the smell of wax, roses and champagne.

"You know what this is, don't you?" Alworth's voice sounded again in her ear. He was whispering.

"I neither know nor care," she also whispered. She wanted to go ahead, but he placed a hand on her shoulder. His hand was warm on her skin.

"It is a *nid d'amour*." A love nest.

The air between them grew thick. It was the scent of roses that befuddled her mind, Pen told herself.

But suddenly her mind turned to jelly, and there was thick, hot honey oozing through her veins. She'd forgotten why she was here and what she wanted. She looked up at him.

The world receded, and there was only Alworth.

His gaze dropped to her mouth. His hand gently brushed her chin.

Entirely without thinking, she stood on tiptoe and touched her lips to his.

Warm and sweet, it rushed through her mind and sang through her veins. Surprisingly gentle. Full of yearning. Then he crushed her to him, and his kiss deepened, kissing her as if there was no tomorrow.

Pen felt drunk.

Drunk on a kiss.

His lips left hers to nibble on her earlobe. "I think," Alworth murmured into her ear, "I think we're not alone."

She looked up at him, blinking. "What?"

He took her arm and led her down the short, narrow hallway, which ended in a scarlet room. A small fountain with a marble statue of Cupid and his arrow graced one corner. In front of it was a scarlet velvet sofa.

On it, in semi-deshabille, was a lady—and the Duke of Rochford, passionately kissing.

Pen gasped.

"Of course," Alworth said in a resigned tone. "The Duke of Rochford and Lady Carrington." She was Lady Whittlesborough's daughter and a widow.

The duke lifted his head. He blinked in drunken confusion when he saw Pen.

"Is that you, Princess?"

CHAPTER 25

*P*en felt her entire world reel.

She wasn't entirely sure whether that was because she'd kissed Alworth, or because she finally stood in front of Marcus.

Who'd been kissing a lady in a flimsy gown, sitting on his lap, pouting seductively. Marcus leaned back against the sofa; his lips twisted into a cynical smile, as though he found the situation of the four of them caught in a love nest amusing.

Pen's chest rose and fell under her laboured breathing.

No one spoke. Only the water in the fountain tinkered.

Having finally found Marcus, after years of yearning, Pen did the only sensible thing one could do in this situation. She tore her arm from Alworth's grasp and rushed back through the tapestry door, elbowing her way through the crowd in the ballroom until she reached the garden. The fresh night air cooled her overheated cheeks. She dropped on her knees and searched with trembling fingers for the leather satchel, which the footman had deposited behind the bush.

It did not make any sense whatsoever, but she urgently

needed to change back into her boy's clothes. Immediately, and on the spot.

She needed to talk to Alworth. She wanted Alworth from the club, not the Alworth who'd just kissed her. Alworth from the club could explain what had just happened. He would shrug everything away with a charming smile. If she turned back into Pen Kumari, they could discuss things reasonably and everything would go back to the way it used to be.

It would undo the kiss.

It would undo that look in his eyes.

Maybe it could undo what she'd seen with Marcus.

She would tell him it had all been a mistake.

Her knees still wobbled as she thought of the kiss.

It made no sense at all, least of all to her, that she needed to be wearing men's clothes to talk to him. But that was how she felt. She couldn't talk to him like that, in her petticoats. Not after she'd kissed him.

Pen managed to sneak by Charlotte and the other guests into an unoccupied chamber and changed her clothes. She took off the braids and flowers on her head and tied, with trembling fingers, her hair back to the simple tail that Pen Kumari wore.

When she felt the familiar breeches close upon her legs, she felt her confidence return.

Thus clad, she had the courage to step up to Alworth. She re-entered the ballroom and found him conversing with Charlotte as though nothing had happened.

Her face fell when she saw her. "Pen. Really?" she said with a sad undertone.

Pen felt a pang of remorse.

She nodded curtly at Alworth.

"Pen." There was resignation in his voice. "I certainly did not expect you to show up at this hour."

"Neither did I." She grabbed a glass of champagne and gulped it down. "I need to talk to you. Alone."

Charlotte pursed her lips in disapproval. "I will go look for William, then." She threw Alworth a quelling look and left for the card room.

"There was no need for you to change into your boy's clothes," Alworth said. "You know, I've known about your charade from the moment we met, from the moment you hurtled into me."

She listened with bewilderment. "You helped me into White's knowing I was a woman?"

Alworth grinned. "Naturally."

Pen digested this. "I thought you'd figured it out later, when you read the story about my parents in the papers. Why did you not say anything earlier?"

"And ruin my primary source of amusement and entertainment?"

"Is that what I have been to you? Amusement and entertainment?" She fixed her dark eyes on him.

He shifted uncomfortably. "It certainly hasn't been boring."

"No," Pen whispered. "It certainly hasn't been that."

Silence settled between them.

Their conversation was every bit as awkward as she'd feared it'd be. The kiss loomed between them. She felt the heat rise again in her cheeks at the mere thought of it.

"And now?" Alworth regarded her carefully. "Did you want to tell me something?"

Pen struggled with the words. "Imagine, my guardian is here." She spoke as if Alworth hadn't been present when they'd met Marcus.

"Is he, indeed? Well, then I take it all your problems are solved in one blow."

His expression held a note of mockery. This was not the

Alworth she wanted to talk to. Hard, aloof, with this cold-eyed smile.

She looked away swiftly. "He sent me Charlotte to turn me back into a girl."

Alworth looked at her without blinking. "So I gather."

She could not, for the life of her, interpret that immobile countenance of his. "I—I should probably go talk to him," she stammered.

"Yes, do. The man seems to have a propensity to disappear. You wouldn't want to lose him again, would you?"

Pen broke away from him.

Marcus had left the card room, with the woman from the scarlet room on his arm. The people melted away in front of them.

Pen boxed her way through the room. Yet the crowd had thickened, and it was getting more difficult to push through.

"Oh! Look who has arrived!" people around her murmured. An excited buzz filled the room.

There, by the entrance, stood a handsome couple. The lady, fashionably dressed in a silver gown, with unruly brown hair, lively eyes, and an amiable smile, stood next to a tall and imposing gentleman, who, with an air of boredom, surveyed the crowd through his quizzing glass.

"Lucy!" Pen heard the shriek as much as everyone else. She needed a moment to realise it came from her. Heads turned in surprise. She scrambled forward. "Lucy, Lucy, Lucy! My dearest, best and only friend."

Completely forgetting that she was dressed in men's clothes, Pen fell around the lady's neck and squeezed her tightly. "How I love you."

The crowd gasped in horrified unison as they watched Pen Kumari, gentleman and gamester, embrace, kiss, and declare his love to the Duchess of Ashmore—in front of her husband and the entire *ton*.

. . .

"Who the blazes are you?" the man beside the duchess enquired in a quietly menacing tone that could've frosted over hell itself.

Alworth, stepped up to the rescue. "This, Your Grace, is my very good friend, Pen Kumari. It seems he has, er, forgotten himself in the exuberant joy of being reunited with your wife."

That didn't necessarily make things any better. The crowd murmured again. The Indian prince? Did he have an *affaire* with the duchess? Since when?

"Do I have to call him out?" the Duke of Ashmore wondered.

"Stand aside, Alworth," said a deep voice. Dead silence fell as Rochford stepped forward. "This is entirely my responsibility. Miss Penelope Reid is my ward."

Pen stared at Marcus and felt the pulse beat in her temple.

So he finally acknowledged her. In front of the entire *ton*.

"Pen?" Lucy murmured into her ear. "Is this really your guardian?"

"Of course I am," Marcus shrugged. "Captain Reid asked me to take on guardianship over his daughter."

The crowd's buzzing increased. The scandal!

"Did I hear right? He is in reality—a she?" a shrill voice, laced with unmitigated delight, asked. It belonged to Lady Carrington, the woman from the secret room. "And she is his ward?"

"By George, I was bested by a girl?" That was the astonished voice of Blackstone.

"Not once, Blackstone, but twice! If one counts the duel, heheh." Forsyth's delight knew no bounds.

"Badly done, Rochford, badly done," Alworth gnashed through his teeth.

Marcus ignored him. "Princess? Shall we go?" He quirked up an eyebrow.

This was when Pen's nerves finally snapped. Where the deuce had he been the entire time? And now he pretended nothing was wrong? Years of hurt, longing and unrequited love bundled themselves up into a ball of rage as she curled her hand into a tight fist and smashed it into his face with a satisfying crack.

The crowd gasped.

Lucy shrieked.

And Pen finally felt something loosen inside her chest.

CHAPTER 26

*C*harlotte had protested. She was Pen's chaperone, and she would take her home to Berkeley Square.

Alworth protested. Pen was not to be taken anywhere at all. She was under his protection. Besides, Pen could very well decide on her own what she wanted.

Marcus nursed his eye. He weakly repeated that he would take care of Pen. He was the guardian, after all. But everyone ignored his protest.

Lucy, however, had wordlessly taken Pen's arm and walked her firmly out of the ballroom. Then she'd whisked her straight to her mansion in Grosvenor Square.

"I don't care what anyone says. But, Pen! In men's clothes? Really?" Lucy clucked her tongue. "And did you have to smash your fist into his face in front of everyone? Mind you, not that he didn't deserve it. I couldn't have done it better and now I feel rather tempted to return right away to blacken his other eye. That blackguard!"

Lucy bundled up her hand to a fist and hit the air. "Except, now you can never show your face in polite society again. And you know I do not care a tuppence about anyone's reputation." Lucy groaned. "Really, Pen. Why, why, *why* didn't you come to me to begin with?"

Why indeed?

Pen was back in petticoats again. They were sitting in the blue drawing room with its delicate Italian furniture, which Pen might've admired, if she hadn't felt so miserable. She crumpled up the handkerchief Lucy had given her. She'd not needed it.

"Of all the people, why does that terrible man have to be your guardian? Pen, I'm so sorry!"

"I did not know about his identity myself until recently." Pen felt exhausted.

The Duke of Ashmore leaned against the mantlepiece of the fireplace, still dressed in his evening clothes. "My love, I can certainly not complain that going out for a mere ball is ever a bland affair. One never knows what adventure one is to expect." He took a pinch of snuff. "Let me see if I can correctly interpret the events of the last hour. She is Penelope Reid. A friend from the seminary in Bath. Who, for some kind of reason that eludes me entirely, has been parading about as a man."

"I am certain she has her reasons, Henry," Lucy interceded.

The duke stared at Pen through his quizzing glass. "She is the ward of the scoundrel Rochford. How on earth did you come to have him as a guardian?" He tipped his quizzing glass against his finger. "There is something else. I seem to remember...She is also that friend of yours who jumped into that wishing well, nearly drowning my sister. She's the one who started the entire story, did she not?"

"I beg your pardon." Pen sat up stiffly. "But it was your sister who'd started the entire affair. If she hadn't thrown those coins into the well, I wouldn't have felt inclined to jump after them."

"Do you do that often? Jump into wells, dress up as a man...I even heard about that infamous gambling match in the Perpignol." The duke looked at her, fascinated. "I might have been tempted to place a wager myself—"

"Henry!" Lucy exclaimed.

He lifted his hands.

Pen glared at him. "To answer your question: Yes, I tend to do that often. I would do it again, any time. Because I would have you know the match was solely to defend Lucy's honour."

Lucy blinked. "My honour? What do you mean?"

Pen told them about the incident with Blackstone.

"It looks like I need to call him out." Ashmore frowned.

"Nonsense, no one is calling anyone out." Lucy jumped up to pour some tea. "Sit down and have some tea. It will calm us all down. Then we can discuss what to do with Pen, for it is a most vexing situation."

"Thank you, my dear, but I will leave you to discuss the issue. I have a certain matter to look into regarding Blackstone." He strolled out of the drawing-room.

"I love him to bits, but sometimes he can be obstinate," Lucy confided to Pen. "It's that dukely streak in him. Honour, responsibility, and all that. But now," she set down her teacup, "tell me the entire story from the moment you left the seminary."

Pen did so, leaving out the incident with the kiss with Alworth.

Lucy sighed. "What are we to do now? Your reputation is in tatters. It doesn't help that Rochford is your guardian. On the contrary, this is probably the true scandal. It turns out that the wicked duke has a beautiful ward, who's even a princess with a mysterious past, and he's kept it a secret all those years. Why would that be? The printing press will run out of ink printing this scandal sheet."

"You don't really think so, do you?" Pen pulled on her lower lip.

Lucy groaned. "I can see the headlines: 'Indian Princess Masquerading as a Boy Reveals Herself to be the Ward of London's Wicked Duke.'" She giggled. "After she's infiltrated White's, called out a lord to a duel, and won against a hardened gamester in a match of cards. Well done, Pen! I am proud of you, truly."

Pen smiled weakly.

"But you planting him a facer was one of the best things I've experienced in a long time. I am very cross with that man. I remember very well how you suffered back at the seminary, waiting to hear from him. You were always watching the street and never left the window in the library."

Pen leaned her dark head against Lucy's shoulder.

The door opened, and the butler entered. "The Duke of Rochford, Your Grace."

"Speaking of the devil." Lucy jumped up.

Pen wrung her hands. "I don't want to see him. I don't want to talk to him. Ever."

"I don't blame you. But Pen. Think. You've been waiting for him for years, and scoured London for him, and now he's finally here, and you don't want to talk to him?"

Pen didn't understand it herself. She wanted to run away, stick her head in the sand and pretend none of it ever happened.

The duke sauntered into the room, his hair dishevelled, his necktie loose, and aside from sporting a purple-black eye, he seemed sober.

"Good morning, ladies." He gave a small bow. "Duchess?" His smile was crooked.

Lucy nodded frostily. "I shall sit over there—" she pointed to an armchair by the window, "sewing." Lucy, who never sewed, picked up an embroidery ring, sat in the armchair and stabbed the cloth with her needle.

Marcus and Pen inspected each other in silence.

"I am sorry for the black eye." Pen finally said. "But I am not sorry that I hit you." She crossed her arms.

"I suppose I deserved it." He raked a hand through his hair and slouched into a chair with a sigh. "I thought I'd done my duty when I dropped you off at that school."

"All those years, you might've written a word or two. Or visited me. Or sent me a package with sweets and books. Or allow me to stay during the holidays with you, in London, or wherever you were all this time—" Pen's voice sounded more and more damning.

Lucy, from the window, made assenting noises but did not raise her head from her embroidery.

"I am a hideous guardian," Marcus agreed. "A wastrel and a cad."

"A rake and a scallywag," Pen added.

"Scoundrel and blackguard," Lucy contributed from the window.

A smile tugged at his mouth. "Have we exhausted the synonyms yet?"

Pen racked her brain for more but drew a blank. She'd been prepared to battle with him. Not having anything else to say regarding the nature of his awful guardianship, she merely glared at him.

"I want to apologise, Pen. I had no idea you ran away. I thought my lawyer had everything in order and was in regular contact with you. You must believe me. It was only when Fariq found me and told me what you'd been up to that I, er—"

"Remembered me," Pen finished his sentence with a scowl.

"Not precisely in those terms, but well." He cleared his

throat. "It appeared you were doing rather well on your own anyhow." He shrugged.

"To sum it up: when you were finally reminded of Pen's existence, you did nothing at all," Lucy's censorious voice came from the window. "Only to declare later to all and sundry that you were her guardian. You might as well have shouted it from the moon. Couldn't you have kept your mouth shut when it really mattered? Pen's reputation is in tatters."

A flush of red crawled over his neck. "I was foxed. I didn't think."

"Obviously." Lucy lifted her needle as if she intended to stab him. "But I suppose you can't tell someone who doesn't care about his reputation to care about someone else's." Pen had never seen her so angry.

Marcus had no reply to that.

"You know, I used to worship the ground you walked on," Pen said quietly into the silence.

Lucy looked at her with a worried frown between her eyes.

"Damnation. I know." He pulled at his already loose cravat.

"No, I think you don't," Pen said softly. "I yearned myself sick at school. I loved you with all the fibre, all the heart and soul a young girl is capable of. I still do."

"You do?" He blinked, dazed. He opened the mouth, then closed it with a snap when he realised they had an audience.

The Duke of Ashmore stood in the open door.

Behind him was Viscount Alworth.

Both had heard Pen's last declaration.

"This seems to be an inopportune time." Ashmore turned to Alworth, who looked grim. "Rochford. I believe Alworth has something to discuss with you. My study is available should you require privacy."

Marcus shrugged and waved a hand. "Might as well discuss it here."

"This is unorthodox," Alworth said. "But very well. This entire business has been unorthodox since the very first. As Miss Reid's guardian, albeit absent most of the time, it may have slipped your attention as to what your ward has been up to these past few weeks. I hold myself partially responsible for having enabled, if not encouraged, some of her adventures. My motivation was curiosity and entertainment. A rather base motivation, I admit. I should have known better. I take responsibility for this scandal. There is but one course of action to take and that is to offer my hand in marriage." He hesitated before adding, "Even though the lady's affections seem to be elsewhere."

His eyes bore into hers.

"Very magnanimous of you, Alworth," drawled Rochford. "And my role here is to give permission?"

Pen wrung her hands in her lap. "Why?"

Alworth quirked up a corner of his mouth. "Why does Rochford have to give his permission? Or why am I proposing marriage?"

"Do you want to marry me, at all? Would it ever have occurred to you to propose if I hadn't caused this scandal? What about Letty Mountroy? Aren't you engaged to her?"

All heads turned to Alworth. He shook his head. "I never proposed to Miss Mountroy."

Pen did not turn her gaze from him. "You wouldn't marry me at all if I hadn't drawn you into this scrape."

"She might have a point there, Alworth," the Duke of Ashmore commented.

"Oh, for heaven's sake, Henry, give the poor man a chance to reply," Lucy interjected. "Alworth?"

Alworth put a finger into his cravat and pulled at it. "Naturally, I feel responsible. I could've quenched all this in the bud at our very first meeting. Instead, I encouraged you to continue your masquerade. And one thing led to another."

"You played with me."

Again, he hesitated. "I wouldn't call it that, precisely. But, yes, you provided some entertainment. But gradually I grew to feel responsible for you. I still do. I am honest in my proposal. And we did kiss." He smiled vaguely.

"Well, there we are." The Duke of Ashmore threw up his hands.

Lucy gasped and clasped her hands. "Oh, did you! Pen!"

But Pen mulled over his words. "You're wrong, you know. It is not for you to take responsibility for my actions. It is mine, entirely," she said in a low voice. "As for my affections…"

Her voice wobbled, then failed as she looked at Marcus. A confusion had settled over her that fogged up her mind. Marcus, whom she'd loved her entire life. Alworth, whose intense eyes caused a fluttering in her stomach and a tightening in her chest, and her words to get all warbled.

"I don't want your sacrifice," she finally whispered.

Alworth frowned. "This isn't a matter of sacrifice. But of doing the honourable thing and of saving what can be saved."

Somehow, this made Pen feel even more wretched.

Lucy wrung her hands. "I am certainly no stickler for reputation, having had none myself before Ashmore married me, so it seems quite outrageous of me to say so. But you are my friend, Pen. A sister, even. And I care deeply for you. Alworth is right. You can, of course, not marry. I take it, once you receive your inheritance, that you have enough funds to get by for some time…"

"Several years," Rochford agreed.

"…and then what? You know how they are. Society will not accept you. Not after all this. The only way out of this muddle is if you marry."

Pen looked unhappily at her friend.

Marcus cleared his throat. "Well. If she won't have him, I suppose it's up to me to come up to scratch." He flashed a crooked smile at Pen. "Marry me?"

There it was. The moment she'd so desired her entire life.

She did not dare to look at Alworth. Somehow, looking at him caused a pain in her heart that she'd rather not feel. She didn't understand the turmoil inside her. Alworth was a stranger. But Marcus—she knew him. He knew her. He'd known her parents. He was her guardian. She'd always wanted to marry him.

He felt safe.

With a big breath, she whispered, "Very well."

CHAPTER 27

*P*en was sitting with Marcus in a carriage on the way to Gretna Green.

After she'd agreed to marry him, Marcus had taken his hat and left.

They'd discussed the matter of a small wedding, with only the witnesses present. This, Lucy insisted, wouldn't do.

"I will organise a small wedding breakfast for you," she decided. "Arabella and Birdie and their families have to attend at the very least, don't you think?" She tipped a finger on her nose. "And Miss Hilversham. Speaking of which, our old teachers, Miss Weston and Miss Elton, too. As for a wedding dress, I have a gorgeous confection that we can have altered..."

Pen had listened to her friend and not said anything at all.

That evening, Marcus had returned and asked to talk to Pen alone.

"I don't know about you, but I'd rather not have this turned into a big fuss," he told her. "Should we go to Gretna Green and get it done and over with?"

"What do you mean, right away?"

He bowed. "Right away."

Pen thought it was a good idea. Get it done and over with. That did not sound too romantic, but she was of the same frame of mind that she'd rather not have a big fuss made at their wedding.

After she put on a bonnet and pelisse and picked up a reticule, she told Lucy that Marcus was taking her for a drive. She felt utterly miserable lying to Lucy like that.

"Enjoy yourself, dear," Lucy said, looking up with a quick smile.

Pen, who'd been half-way out of the door, choked. She turned, ran back and gave Lucy a fierce hug.

"You know, if you happen to decide to drive somewhat further than Hyde Park, further to the north, I would completely understand that," Lucy murmured into her ear.

Pen pulled back, astonished. "How did you know?"

Lucy smiled. "I wasn't born yesterday, you know."

Pen gave her a tremulous smile.

She almost changed her mind and had that wedding breakfast at Ashmore Hall after all.

So now she found herself in the carriage with Marcus, going north.

For most of the journey, Marcus had been reticent. Pen, never much of a talker herself, had leaned her heated head against the carriage window and wondered why she felt a pain in her heart even though she finally got what she'd always wanted.

Marcus leaned his curly head against the back of the seat, asleep. She studied his pale face, which showed the signs of his dissipated lifestyle.

He'd always behaved in a polite, rather distant manner towards her. Too polite, she thought. Too distant. It was as though his thoughts were always elsewhere. Now and then she caught him staring at her intently. Only to look away quickly when her eyes met his.

She heard, through Lucy, that Alworth was to leave for India soon. That should not come as any surprise, for he'd told her of his plans from the moment they met.

The carriage rattled through the countryside, and rain prattled against the window. Somehow that suited Pen's mood. A happy bride felt otherwise, she assumed.

"Why did you never come looking for me?" Pen asked him. She knew that, even though his eyes were closed, that he wasn't really asleep. "Was it because you'd forgotten about me? Or because you were ashamed of me?"

A muscle twitched in his jaw. His green eyes opened. "Never ashamed, Princess. Never so."

"Then, why?"

He studied her face. "How much do you remember your mother?"

"Mama?" Pen thought. Her face, like so many things from her childhood in India, turned into a hazy blur. "I think she was rather pretty."

"Rather pretty?" He uttered a hollow laugh. "She was beautiful." The way he said it, there was an undercurrent of something in his voice that made Pen listen up.

"Tell me about her," Pen said.

"She was the most enchanting woman I've ever seen in my entire life. And I have seen my share of beautiful women. Then I met Adita." There was pain in his eyes. "John was posted to Jaipur. I accompanied him. It was like a fairy tale. And your mother a fairy tale princess."

Pen's breath came heavily as the full impact of what he revealed to her sank in. "You loved her."

At first, she thought he would not answer. When he did,

there was a world full of pain in his voice. "Oh yes, I did. This wasted heart is very much capable of love. The real thing. But she chose John. Not me. Never me."

"You loved my mother," Pen repeated numbly, not fully comprehending. "And then she died."

His voice cracked. "I couldn't save them. I couldn't save her."

Pen remembered how he'd pulled her out of the rubble. Somehow, she'd been unhurt. He'd set her aside and then went looking for her mother. Who'd died with her father. Even in death, they lay in each other's arms.

She remembered Marcus, his face full of tears, how he'd held her mother's dusty and broken dead body, rocking her.

Pen had howled. She'd clung to him. And he'd promised he'd take care of her forever.

Here she was, on the way to Gretna Green, to marry Marcus.

"You loved my mother," she repeated.

"You are a spitting image of her. Do you know? Now even more so than when you were younger. It is—difficult to look at you. To see her likeness in your face, and yet it is not her. It is uncanny." He swallowed. "I do like you, Pen. Very much so. But you have to forgive me. I could not, for a long while, bear to look at you."

There was stark sorrow on his face. "I suppose this is why I chose to break contact with you. It was—still is—easier for me to drown in alcohol and opium."

Silence settled in the carriage as Pen digested what he just told her.

Her voice shook. "What about Charlotte Wentwood?"

He blinked at her. "Who?"

Another realisation punched her in the gut. "You never sent her." She closed her eyes. "You never sent Charlotte Wentwood. You're not my sponsor."

"Sponsor?"

Of course he was not.

"You were never my sponsor. For the ball. For the season. You never sent Charlotte to turn me into a girl. I thought—I thought you sent her. Which was the only reason I agreed to go along with her as she tried to turn me into a lady."

He cocked his head to one side. "Should I have? After Fariq told me of your masquerade, I thought you did rather well on your own. That match with Blackstone. I taught you well, didn't I?" A ghost of a smile flitted over his face. "I thought it best not to interfere."

Or not to care.

He hadn't come to the ball because of her, either, but because of the woman with the rouged cheeks, Lady Carrington.

A good guardian would've not only picked her up from the seminary when her time there was over, he would've obtained a chaperone for her, given her a season, made sure she was taken care of.

"It doesn't matter." She stared blindly out of the window. Then she laughed.

"I am glad you can find some amusement in this situation," Marcus said.

"I am just finding this odd," Pen said. "My friend Arabella once made a wish that each of us, her friends, marry a duke. That must have been a powerful wish, for here I am, on the way to marrying one. Except—" She looked up, realisation dawning in her eyes. "Except I just realised I don't want to."

It hit her like lightning. Alworth. It had always been Alworth. He'd been her guardian angel in so many ways. In his sleepy, sarcastic, charming, bullying way. He'd been her true friend all along, and she'd never seen it. He'd gone along with her antics, even though he'd seen through her. He'd guided and protected her. He'd wanted to marry her, even. To save her reputation.

He'd been the only person who ever saw and accepted her for who she really was. He'd never made assumptions based on her appearance. Whether she was Indian, British, prince, princess, street boy, gentleman, gambler, lady, all or none of it—he was the only one who understood that the face you showed to the world did not necessarily have to match up with the reality of who you were inside. He'd seen and understood the confusion inside her. Maybe that was because Alworth himself wore a mask. That of the superficial dandy. They were more alike than different.

She always thought she needed Marcus to understand who she really was.

She couldn't have been more mistaken.

She needed precisely no one to help her realise she was Pen. Just Pen.

Something dreadful squeezed in her chest. Hot, tight, unbearably burning. She choked.

"Is anything the matter?" Marcus sat up in alarm.

"I'm f-f-fine." Something hot rolled over her cheeks. Something unfamiliar. Something she'd not done in a very long time.

For the first time since that terrible day she'd lost her parents, the stone that was lodged in her chest loosened, and Penelope Reid cried.

THE CARRIAGE HAD HALTED BY THE WAYSIDE, AND THE DRIVER groaned. "Are we to continue on to Scotland now, or not, Your Grace?"

Pen had descended from the carriage and looked over the barren, wind-swept fields. They were in the middle of nowhere. If they continued down that road, they would reach Scotland. She turned and looked the other way, the one going south. That was the road to Alworth.

Marcus took out the grass blade from his mouth and threw it into the wind. "Tell me when you've made up your mind, Princess. As I said, I'd marry you. I owe it to your parents, after all. The last thing I can do for them." He stared down the road, the wind swept his hair across his high forehead. "I am rubbish as a guardian. You know I'd be even more so as a husband. It will be a marriage of convenience. But you will be taken care of in all ways. It is an oath I would keep with my soul."

She turned to him. "In all ways, but one. You will never love me. You'd marry me out of obligation and guilt. You'd marry me not because you see me, Pen. But because you see my mother in me. Because you still love her."

His silence was affirmation.

Pen nodded.

"We proceed, then?"

"No." The wind blew into her face, and it felt good on her swollen eyes. Finally, she knew what she wanted. "I want to go back. To London."

"To do what, exactly?"

"To catch Alworth before he journeys to India."

A CRUSH OF PEOPLE FILLED THE EAST INDIA DOCKS, ALONG with their trunks, boxes, and crates. Everyone was in each other's way as passengers waited to board their ships. Finding Alworth in the crowd was like finding a sardine in a sea of herrings.

Pen dropped her shoulders. "It's hopeless."

She rubbed her nose. It smelled of salty seawater, rotten fish, and sewage.

Marcus grabbed a sailor. "Which ship to the East Indies?"

The sailor shrugged. "They're all East Indiamen."

Marcus turned to Pen. "Do you remember which ship is his?"

She racked her brain. "It's the *Adelaide*." He'd mentioned it once in a conversation at the club. How long ago that was.

"The *Adelaide*'s there." The sailor jerked his head towards a massive merchant ship that was loading cargo. People stood in line to board the ship.

Pen caught a flash of pink on the front deck. There was only one man who wore pink like that. She squinted. "I think he's on deck. Over there."

She ran. But the dock was jammed full of people, so progress was difficult. She mowed into a man who dropped all the trunks.

"Oy. Watch it!"

"I'm so sorry. But I have to get on the ship." She boxed her way forward. "I need to get on the ship."

"Tickets and papers, please," an officer said in a bored voice, and held out his hand.

"I just need to talk to someone. Please."

"Only passengers with tickets are allowed on board. Move aside, please. Next?"

Marcus pulled her aside. "You can't just walk on board like that."

Pen grasped his arm. "If you ever, ever cared a bit about me, and I mean *me*, and not my mother, or whatever image of my mother you have in mind. Just me. Pen. Then you will help me get on board."

"Do you really want that, Princess?" He looked at her searchingly.

"I am certain."

"How certain?"

"I love him." She uttered a choked laugh. "I am a fool that

I did not notice earlier. But it is true. I must have loved him for a while. I—I just did not realise it until you came along."

He gave a wistful smile. "At least one good thing that my unworthy self helped you with. Very well." He stared at her as if to memorise her face. "I am so very sorry for everything. I truly am."

Pen nodded.

"Are you moving on, or not?" The impatient voice of a man sounded behind them.

"Marcus?" Her eyes sought his.

"Go find your happiness, Princess," he said before he pulled himself up to haughty heights. "Do you know who you are addressing? I am the Duke of Rochford. And I want to buy a ticket for a passage in the best cabin. Now."

The officer replied, flustered. "That isn't possible, Your Grace."

Marcus raised an eyebrow. "The word impossible is not a part of my vocabulary. Lead me to your captain, if you please. Immediately."

"But Your Grace…"

As they argued, no one noticed that Pen sidled herself past the officer and walked up the plank. First slowly, then faster, until she ran the last bit.

She was on board the *Adelaide.*

THE SEA BREEZE RUFFLED ALWORTH'S CAREFULLY COIFFED hair. Ice cold drops of sea water sprayed into his face. It was deuced chilly on deck.

He clasped the rail with his hands and looked back as the docks grew smaller and smaller until the mass of people consisted of teeming dots. Like ants.

His luggage had been brought to his cabin, a luxurious,

spacious suite that would be his home for the next six months or more. The trip would go around the Cape of Good Hope, to Madagascar and then on to Bombay. It was going to be the adventure of a lifetime. Before he'd met Pen, he'd looked forward to this trip. Now the prospects of the voyage left him listless and wan.

He drummed his fingers against the rails.

She would be married to that wastrel by now. She was the Duchess of Rochford.

He couldn't get her face out of his mind. Her narrow face with huge eyes, fringed with thick, black lashes. The quirk of her mouth when she smiled. The tilt of her head when she listened to him.

He couldn't forget that odd look on her face, the one she'd given him when she'd agreed to marry her cursed guardian. He could've sworn she hadn't wanted to.

Then why the deuce had she said yes to him?

Why had he let her go?

But after he'd heard that she loved him, always did, it had felt like a piece of his heart had been torn out. But one doesn't commonly acknowledge things like that.

"You love her," Serena, who always saw too much, had said with an odd smile on her face.

Balderdash.

He felt himself sweat despite the cold air.

This wasn't love, was it? That unbearable aching, yearning of his soul. It was different from what he'd felt towards Serena. That had been puppy love compared to this.

Surely, it would go away soon. Surely, one could cure it? Like a sickness.

It will heal. With time, the hole will heal over, and he'll be perfectly fine. He'll get over this fit of the blue-devils. He'll be his smiling, charming old self again, except there'll be an emptiness inside that nothing in the world will fill.

Alworth swore.

He really had rotten luck with love.

It would be good to be in Bengal for a while. Everything in London would remind him of her. Get rid of the memory of that face. Get rid of the image he carried of her in his heart. Dash it, now he even imagined he heard her voice.

"Alworth."

He blinked.

There she stood.

In a grass green coat, her cheeks red from the wind, her eyes sparkling with tears.

It was a beautiful vision.

So real.

She hurled herself at him and sobbed into his coat.

Slowly, it dawned on him that maybe this wasn't just his imagination. His arms clamped around her like she was his only anchor.

"What the blazes, Pen," he whispered hoarsely.

"If you go to India, then I will go with you." She sobbed into his coat. "And if you don't want me, then I will rent a cabin next to yours and just stay there and look at you from afar."

He pressed her tightly to him, his mind whirling, his nose full of the smell of her hair, of honeysuckle.

Alworth, Viscount, dandy, Nonpareil, charmer of the *ton*, always so elegant in manner and speech, was struck dumb.

"I am so, so, so sorry," Pen blabbed. "It was you; it was always you. Well, maybe not always, because I did insist on running after Marcus all the time, didn't I. I am such a pig-widgeon. I don't know when I stopped caring for him, but I am certain I just loved an image of him I had since I was a child, an image that wasn't true. But it was so hard to let go of *wanting* it to be true, you know what I mean?"

She lifted her wet face to him, and he'd never seen anything so beautiful in his life.

"So when I finally saw him after all this time, the old Pen couldn't just let go. He was never the man I had created in my mind. That was a fantasy, a beautiful one, but it gave me comfort. Marcus," she shook her head, "never loved me. He always loved my mother. I look like her, so maybe he likes me a bit because of that, but that is all.

"It was always you; you know. Your friendship, kindness, loyalty. When I am with you, it feels as though I don't have to pretend. Which is ironic because most of the time I was disguised as a boy. But you saw through that. You saw me for who I was. Always. Even when I was a brat, and a nuisance and a gudgeon, and I always fell into some sort of pickle or other from which you tried to help me. And you were always s-s-so patient with me." Pen sobbed. "And will you please, please say something? Otherwise, I will throw myself into the Thames right away and disappear forever."

"Pen. Penelope Reid. Will you be quiet so that I can finally kiss you?"

Her eyes grew big and round. "Oh yes, please!"

He pressed her to him and kissed her like a drowning man. He tasted the sweetness of her lips, the salt of her tears. Then the kiss softened and grew achingly tender.

"Ahem." A voice behind them cleared his throat.

Alworth and Pen strove apart and stared into the stern face of the ship's captain.

"I have been told there is a marriage to be performed. By orders of the Duke of Rochford. Who happens to be a good friend of mine." The captain's stern face melted into a smile.

"Do you want to?" Alworth looked down tenderly on her. "Marry me?"

She leaned her head against his shoulder. "Oh yes, I do. Very much."

The sun broke through the heavy grey clouds at that moment, throwing a double rainbow above.

Deep in the turquoise waters of the wishing well in Paradise Row, the last of four coins flared up with a bright glimmer before it extinguished forever.

ABOUT THE AUTHOR

 Sofi was born in Vienna, grew up in Seoul, studied Comparative Literature in Maryland, U.S.A., and lived in Quito with her Ecuadorian husband. When not writing, she likes to scramble about the countryside exploring medieval castle ruins, which she blogs about here. She currently lives with her husband, 3 trilingual children, a sassy cat, and a cheeky dog in Europe.

Get in touch and visit Sofi at her Website, on Facebook or Instagram!

🅵 facebook.com/sofilaporteauthor
🐦 twitter.com/Sofi_Laporte
🅾 instagram.com/sofilaporteauthor

Made in the USA
Middletown, DE
27 September 2023